Rebecca F. John is from Pwll, a village on the South Wales coast. She studied English and Creative Writing at Swansea University. Her stories have shortlisted for a number of awards. She works as a ski instructor.

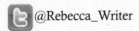 @Rebecca_Writer

www.rebeccafjohn.com

Clown's Shoes

Clown's
Shoes

Rebecca F. John

PARTHIAN

Parthian, Cardigan SA43 1ED

www.parthianbooks.com

First published in 2015

© Rebecca F. John 2015

ISBN 978-1-910409-67-1

Editor: Susie Wild

Cover design by Robert Harries

Typeset by Elaine Sharples

Printed and bound by Gomer Press, Llandysul, Wales

Published with the financial support of the Welsh Books Council

British Library Cataloguing in Publication Data

A cataloguing record for this book is available from the British Library.

For my parents, who never denied me a book

Contents

English Lessons

The lighthouse casts a long wedge of deep, syrupy darkness down the stretch of the jetty and into the sea. The rest of the harbour is washed in a silvery glaze. Scarf pulled up over her nose, Eunkyung steps secretly around the widest curve of the lighthouse's circumference. From Narae's house it is only a small cylindrical lump at the water's edge, but here, near its base, it is so vast and solid that it seems possible the whole world might extend outwards from this one fixed point. Eunkyung tips her head back and traces its thrust into the sky. Lit by a moon which lounges low over the village, the red and white stripes are two different shades of grey.

Keeping to the shadows, she finds a place to sit on the harbour wall. High above the tilting line where the stone gives way to the water, she swings her legs in the empty black air. Below, the waves bubble against the rocks before retreating with cheerful popping sounds, and Eunkyung practises her smile.

Everyone wants her to smile here.

As she grins and relaxes, grins and relaxes, she inhales the rich, hideous smell of the sea and considers the urge to jump in on a scale, from one to ten, as Narae has taught her to. Whenever she feels sad or homesick or confused, Narae has explained, she is to picture in her mind a big ruler, and assign the strength of that feeling a number. Only once that is decided will she be able to find a way to move it down towards the 'one' end. One – not much of a feeling at all, but more like the tickle an insect makes

1

when it lands on your skin then takes immediately off again – is the aim. And there must be an aim, Narae has insisted, because that is the way Eunkyung will learn to feel at home here – by trying hard at it.

Tonight, though, sitting in the snow with the misty tentacles that rise towards the shore winding around her, sucking her in, Eunkyung is hovering between an eight and a nine. The date and the hour are making her feel more lost than she has in months and, though she knows it is not possible, right now it seems that if she could just find the courage to slip below the water's surface, she could swim all the way back to Seoul.

September 21st
The plane descended as smoothly as liquid. Eunkyung pressed her forehead to the window, straining to see around the long white nose of the fuselage. Since the seatbelt sign had blinked on, she had been expecting the city to emerge from below, bright and chaotic as a circus ring and sprawling forever outwards. London, she knew, was one of the most famous cities in the world. As the wheels touched down and the plane shuddered along the runway, though, there were only the lights of the airport, sparking sadly against the wet sky, as small and insignificant and similar as specks of rain caught under lamplight.

She looked down the rows of seats. A hundred dark-haired domes showed over the grey headrests. Specks of rain, Eunkyung thought: all of them. She couldn't imagine how Narae would know her.

Stepping towards the plane door, she tried to dream up something big and silent enough to cloak London, but she could not distract herself from the idea that she was on the wrong flight, that Narae would not appear to collect her. She glanced at her in-flight nanny. She would not ask this small, leathery woman, who meant business and spoke in clipped, formal Korean. Eunkyung, immediately frightened of her, had chanced only one sentence since they'd met. 'How will we find my auntie?'

In response, her nanny had simply tutted and returned to her reading, which had made Eunkyung think she did not know.

As they filed past the stewardess, Eunkyung thought of asking her. She was blue-eyed and red-lipped and had perhaps the friendliest face Eunkyung had ever seen. 'Where am I?' she wanted to say. 'This can't be London.' But her grasp of English was poor. She was only truly confident with *hello*, and *thank you*, and *my name is* …

'Hello,' she said to the stewardess, but instantly she could see she had it wrong this time. It wasn't the same, arriving and leaving.

The stewardess frowned. 'Oh, no,' she said. 'It's not *hello* now. It's *goodbye*.' She lifted her hand and waved it, inches from Eunkyung's face. 'Goodbye,' she sung.

Eunkyung copied the sounds. 'Goodbye.' They sounded sticky on her tongue.

'Yes,' the stewardess said, clapping her tiny hands together. 'Goodbye.'

Eunkyung ducked through the oval door onto the clanky steps and stuck out her tongue to taste the damp air. It was both warm and cold, and seemed to be settling in little orbs all over her skin. She gripped the handrail and descended the steps. Funny, she thought, that goodbye was the first thing this country had taught her.

But Eunkyung did not have time to grow gloomy about it, because from the second her feet met the ground it was as though she'd dropped out of the sky and into a film in fast forward. The nanny steered her through the airport like a race-car driver; they whipped her luggage, one bag each, off the rotating belt; they left a distorted blur in the darkened shop windows. And less than thirty minutes later they were standing in the empty, bleached belly of the airport building, positioned opposite a couple Eunkyung did not recognise.

'This is Narae,' said the nanny. 'And this is David, your auntie's husband.'

Narae was a round-faced, round-bellied character, whose smile gaped like a letterbox. She strode forward and put her hands on Eunkyung's shoulders. 'I'm really glad to meet you,' she said, in English, and Eunkyung wondered whether she had forgotten how to speak Korean. She'd been gone such a long time – since before Eunkyung was born. As David lifted the bags and they turned towards the sliding exit doors, though, she heard Narae exchange a few rushed words with the nanny. She still had her Korean. She just wasn't going to share it with her niece.

Walking into the night, Eunkyung tried to think of a reason why. The only one that came to mind was that her auntie didn't want her. After all, Narae had inherited Eunkyung. She didn't come with any money, or property, or promises. She wasn't the brightest girl in her class, or a talented sportswoman. She didn't even excel at music, as her mother had in childhood. She was simply something Chanmi had left behind, which could not be abandoned.

She might as well have been her mother's antique piano.

In the car, Narae twisted around in her seat and crinkled her eyes as though she was smiling. 'Why don't you sleep for a while?'

Eunkyung did not want to explain that she couldn't understand; why she couldn't understand. She was tired. Instead she fastened her seatbelt and stared out through the window as the car swooped away from the airport. It was not raining now, but it ought to be: the sky was flabby and heavy and looked full enough to burst. Rolling minutes had passed before Eunkyung realised that those elusive, hulking shapes she'd identified as clouds were actually mountains. She hadn't known whether there

4

would be mountains or not. The whole country was a mystery to her: how big it was; what it would look like.

Almost as much of a mystery as the two people in the front of the car.

As David spoke his long chains of flat words, Eunkyung considered the back of his head. From behind, his narrow shoulders made him look childlike, or ill. His face though was an affable one, made kind by its plainness. His voice, too, was nice. Her eyes closed to it. And as soon as Eunkyung had settled into the easy rhythm of the car on the motorway, they were slowing down, curling around and around corkscrew roads, and stopping on the smallest street she had ever visited. She counted the houses as she got out – *yeol dul*. A light remained on in only one: a faint, yellow blush on the night's face. A shadow moved across the window, then shrunk to nothing.

A path laid with thousands of little stones led from the car to the front door. Narae and David picked over them quietly and Eunkyung, following, stole one last long look around. She could see nothing beyond the end of the street but skinny trees, reaching into the clumpy grey clouds like finger bones. Her auntie must not live anywhere near London.

'You'll go there all the time,' Chanmi had said, shoving Eunkyung with a shoulder and smiling. 'Narae lives very close. And it's the most exciting place in the entire world, London. Isn't it, in all the films and the songs?' Chanmi rolled back her head and, shutting her eyes, took a long, wistful breath. Eunkyung could tell she was pretending at it. 'Oh, if I could have visited that city when I was twelve years old…'

But this was not London. Chanmi's stories about Narae had been wrong, then. Or untrue.

As Eunkyung stepped towards the strange black rectangle Narae's door had opened into, she pushed that suspicion far away, and decided instead that Chanmi must have been mistaken. It was her decision to make now that her mother was gone. And her decisions were all bent around thinking only good things; around forgetting that empty block of time in which she had learned, pre-emptively, what it was to be motherless.

December 27th

When she grows so cold she can no longer bear it, Eunkyung stands and walks footprints into the snow. It is crispy underfoot. With each step it spills over the fronts of her boots, shining like the starry sea. She makes patterns in the snow, placing one foot carefully in front of the other, heel to toe. She begins with the number nine, but her promise to Narae weighs on her and she turns it into the wing of a bird. When she has finished, she climbs up onto the wall she had been sitting on, to view it from above, then throws her arms out and flaps them, faster and faster, until she feels laughter uncoiling in her stomach.

November 8th

Narae drove faster than her husband. They dipped down between two walls of thick trees onto the motorway and swerved into the lines of traffic like a spooked horse, and Eunkyung had to grip the sides of her seat to stay upright.

'Don't look so scared,' Narae said. 'I'm a very good driver. I've only ever had three crashes.' Eunkyung nodded. 'Very small ones,' she added. 'Just bumps, really. Anyway, everyone drives like this in Cardiff, you'll see.'

They'd left just after lunch, David waving them off through the kitchen window, his arm sudsy and cartoonish with washing-up liquid. Eunkyung had waved back from the passenger seat, grinning until Narae had reversed off the drive and eased away from the house. She'd been right to like David. He brought Narae cups of tea while she sat in bed some mornings. He made her laugh until her belly hurt. Eunkyung had never seen anyone do either of those things for Chanmi.

'Do you know what Cardiff is?' Narae asked.

'The capital city,' Eunkyung said, in Korean. She knew now, where she was, where the border between the two countries lay.

'Yes. Good,' Narae answered.

This was how they had come to converse, Narae saying the English words in a tender monotone, and Eunkyung answering in her swift Korean to show that she understood, even if she couldn't yet fully respond. It was obvious Narae loved English. She never slipped up and broke into Korean.

'When did you last speak Korean, Auntie?' Eunkyung asked.

'Twenty years ago, nearly,' Narae replied. The answer made Eunkyung sad. She didn't want to stop speaking Korean – not ever. Korean was the only language her mother knew. 'And what happened to your English lessons anyway?' Narae continued. 'You should have had two or three years by now.'

Eunkyung was quiet. She knew Chanmi would have lied to her sister about how often she sent her daughter to school. When middle school started, Chanmi had said, it was going to be different, then she would have to attend every day, but all through elementary school, Eunkyung's mother had hidden her away in their apartment; sometimes for days at a time.

'Let's pretend we're sisters,' she'd say, 'and that we've run away from home, and we can make up all our own rules!' Or, 'Let's imagine we're spies, and that our neighbours are our targets. Let's see what we can find out about them.' And they would play their games, then. They would make-believe that they had found work as fashion designers or magazine editors, and discuss their ideas over coffee. They would swap clothes and saunter up and down the hallway outside the flat, pretending that Chanmi was the child and Eunkyung the mother. They would stay up all night together and watch the city lights grow brighter and brighter until the entire sky shone as brilliantly as the moon.

At night, the sky was always the same dense dark over Narae's house. When Eunkyung looked up at it, she felt like she was gazing into the deepest of waters.

'Now, tell me, in English, what colour you want to dye your hair,' Narae ordered.

Eunkyung had been able to sit on her hair once, but she'd had to cut it in sixth grade, ready for middle school, and now it swung just beneath her ears. She still missed the weight of it hanging down her back, heavy and warm as wool. She'd never even started middle school.

'Pink,' she said.

Narae laughed. 'No, not pink. You have it wrong. Put it into your translator.'

Eunkyung knew the individual letters well; she had learned them on the flight over and practised them at breakfast each morning since. She also knew that 'pink' was the word she wanted. As soon as she'd seen the girl at school with pink hair, she'd stopped Katie in the corridor and typed a question into her translator.

'You can dye it if you want,' Katie told her. 'Course you can.' And because she was nodding as she spoke, Eunkyung knew she was confirming her wish. A nod of the head was enough. Already, though, she had discovered that there were so many words for 'yes'. A teacher had explained, slowly and with many stops and frowns, that this was because some people spoke Welsh as well as English.

Eunkyung held up her translator to Narae and nodded. 'Pink.'

Narae shook her head. 'Blonde,' she said. 'That's as much as I'll allow.' When Eunkyung tried to type in 'blonde' for a translation, she couldn't find the right letters. Perhaps it was another Welsh word. She pushed the translator into her bag.

'Will I have to learn two languages?' she asked, after a pause. 'Two?'

'English *and* Welsh.'

'No,' Narae answered. 'Just one will be enough.'

After that, though, Narae took her hand off the steering wheel each time they flew past a big, blue sign and pointed out how the Welsh word sat above its English translation. Thinking that perhaps, deep down, Narae really did want her to learn this new language, Eunkyung studied the signs all the way to Cardiff. Cardiff came under Caerdydd. Caerdydd, then, was the Welsh. But she said nothing of this to Narae. If the Welsh and the English had been switched, she wouldn't have known. She couldn't see the difference.

Cardiff was smaller than Eunkyung had imagined: the streets were short; the buildings stubby. Compared to Seoul, it looked like a toddling child. All afternoon, Eunkyung watched people stop and gather in rings to talk, or pat each other's shoulders as they crossed paths. And when she sat down at the hairdressers, the woman who draped the towel over her shoulders smiled so easily that Eunkyung thought she must be a friend of Narae's.

She tried to persuade the woman into pink, but Narae corrected her with laughs and confidence, and it was only when she ended up with the 'blonde' that Eunkyung understood it was another word for 'yellow'. She liked it, though. As they walked back to the car in the evening dark, she held her head high and straight, not wanting to ruffle her newly sleeked bob.

They passed a bar where people were dribbling out onto the street, their drinks sloshing over the tops of their glasses and splattering the pavement. Eunkyung gawped, twizzling her head around to get a better view. At her side, Narae whispered, 'Don't stare,' but she couldn't help it. The mounds of white flesh that drooped over the tops of skirts or pressed their way between shirt buttons were mesmerising.

Soon, they turned onto a quieter street, and Eunkyung finally felt bold enough to voice the question she had been storing these past weeks.

'Why didn't you and Chanmi talk anymore?' she asked, her brisk Korean stumbling slightly.

Narae started to walk faster, her miniature feet taking little-girl steps. 'It was difficult,' she said.

'Difficult.' Eunkyung knew that word. It came up all the time at school. She used the English. 'Difficult, why?'

'Because she didn't like my choice of husband, and I didn't like her –'

'Auntie. Please?'

'Okay, okay.' Narae took a deep breath before she moved into the Korean. Her voice seemed to snap out a different sound then; a higher pitch. 'Because she didn't like my choice of husband,' she said slowly, 'and I didn't like her choice of life.'

'What do you mean her "choice of life"?'

'She lived badly,' Narae answered. 'You must know that.'

'She didn't,' Eunkyung countered, taking a careful breath of her own. Chanmi had warned her about these conversations, about saying too much and exposing their most recent 'game'. She had insisted on calling it their game, though Eunkyung had not seen any fun in it, not once. She still didn't.

'I'm sorry, but she did. I watched her do it. She had a bad mind, your mother, and I'm not afraid to say so, because it's true.' Narae let out a loud huff, but did not look at her niece. 'It was her bad mind that led her to bad men.'

'She didn't do that,' Eunkyung said again. 'I never once saw her do that. It was just us. Just me and her, and she liked it… she liked it that way.'

Narae said nothing. As they walked quicker, her breath smoked out of her nose and mouth like an angry dragon's. Her heels stabbed the pavement with sharp clicks.

'She didn't do that,' Eunkyung said again. But Narae didn't say anything. She just kept walking.

December 27ᵗʰ

In her pocket, Eunkyung feels the phone Narae bought her for Christmas buzz again. She will not answer it. The screen-light shines greenly through her pocket and she clamps her hand over it, in case it gives her away. She is not ready to be found yet. She ducks down behind the little stone wall that runs the length of the harbour and presses her back to the cold. It is only then, looking back towards the village, that she sees them – the lights. Above the rows of yellow-headed streetlamps, the long, shifting beams of torches pierce the sky like bands of tiny lighthouses.

Soon after, she hears the voices. They call her name, over and over, chiming out the three soft syllables in tandem, and she pulls into herself, resting her chin on her knees.

That she knows the truth does not make her feel better. That's why she is here, sitting in the snow with feelings that measure a nine on her imaginary ruler: because she cannot reveal her mother's secret, and because she does not know how long it will be before Chanmi appears to reclaim her. Though Eunkyung had begged, Chanmi had not told her where she was going. She had said only that an opportunity had come up, a one-off chance to make them rich and to do something good, and that she had to take it, but that for it to work she had to be dead – in Narae's mind, anyway.

'Why?'

'Because Narae would never allow it,' Chanmi explained, pulling at the ends of Eunkyung's hair, the way she did when she wanted to see her daughter laugh. 'Because Narae would find a way to put a stop to it, if she found out. And I need her to look after you for a while.'

Eunkyung had been too afraid to ask then if her mother was unwell. She had noticed Chanmi rubbing at her stomach lately, though, as if she was in pain. She had noticed, too, that she seemed to be swelling up – around her stomach, her wrists, her

11

ankles. Eunkyung's greatest fear – the one she had voiced the last time she saw her mother, and which has grown with each passing week since – is that something bad will happen; that Chanmi will not come back, one Christmas, as she had promised, and that Eunkyung will never find out why.

The voices are nearing now. Their calls sound at longer intervals. She sees moonlit figures approaching and clustering together. She identifies Narae and David amongst them, then the lady who lives next door. There are other voices she does not know, though, and as her search party runs short of village and converges onto the jetty, she gauges their dark bulks against the squat figure of Narae, who leads them forward like some ragged army.

One by one, their calls drop away, until there is only the dull march of their feet and the salty susurration of the sea.

Narae halts before her and, frowning slightly, opens her mouth to say any one of a hundred unpleasant things. Eunkyung recognises the expression – Chanmi showed it to her often enough – and she knows that good words never follow it. She wonders if Narae realises she shares these shifts of facial muscle with her sister. She wonders, too, if she is glad to share the care of her child.

Eunkyung lifts her head to speak. 'Is it so cold for always?' she asks and, almost right away, Narae smiles and claps her hands together.

'Ah, you used the English,' she says, moving forward and looping her hand under Eunkyung's arm to coax her to stand. 'And no,' she continues. 'Soon enough it will be summer. Warm. Soon enough. Just wait.'

'Yes,' Eunkyung answers. 'I'll wait.' And though she does not understand why, this makes the people nearby laugh, their breath bursting palely on the black air. So she smiles and laughs back at them. 'I'll wait,' she says again. 'I'll wait.'

The Glove Maker's Numbers

'No, Christina,' the woman says. 'Please don't read.'

But already Christina has weighed the book between careful palms and, recognising its solid width, flipped open the covers. She is impatient to find the first words. She knows what they will say, of course, but she wants to see them for herself. To make sure. If they feel right, she thinks, she will know that she is well again.

The pages emit their little whisper as she turns them and she wills them, for once, to shout. *In the beginning. In the beginning.* It seems such an unremarkable way to go about Creation that it is difficult, now, to trust.

'You handed me a Bible,' Christina replies slowly, closing the covers again.

'Oh, she's a funny one today, is she?' The woman raises her brows. 'Just hold it and sit still, please.'

'For how long?'

'Only ten minutes or so.'

Christina begins calculating how many stitches she could sew in ten long minutes, but she can't fit the figures together properly, in the columns they must be stacked into to make a total, and she gives up. It must be tens of thousands. She glances about, looking for shapes that might make numbers reflected in the scrubbed floorboards and the few weak clouds visible through the closed windows. In one particular cloud she finds an enormous figure

13

of five and she pictures herself perched in its rising tail, then, a moment later, balanced on the flat top ledge of a pure white seven. She pictures herself floating away.

This is what she does now with the words she would once have said – she translates them into numbers and lets them linger silently in her mind. That way, no one can tell her they are wrong.

Though maybe this in itself is the Devil's work – to try and hide her thoughts from everyone, God included. She cannot ask anyone about it. That was when things had become hysterical, when she had started mentioning the Devil by name and wondering what she had done to deserve a visitation. That was what had led Daniel to agree – one hand across his chest to balance the other, held cowardly over his eyes – with some stuck-up doctor, though she had begged and begged him not to. Christina met that doctor all of once, and certainly hasn't seen him since he voiced the new and wonderful notion that she was a lunatic.

At least, she can only presume it was a wonderful notion, since everyone seemed so keen to believe it.

Now, the general consensus is that she is better, recovered, no longer a lunatic. And though this opinion hasn't been so readily accepted, Christina has vowed not to attempt to persuade anyone of it. Let them believe what they will. She doesn't feel any different.

'What will I do for ten minutes?' Christina asks, though she isn't expecting an answer beyond 'be photographed'. It is how things are here. Ten minutes for this. Ten minutes for that. Every task given its title and not one requiring the use of a brain. It had not taken Christina long to learn to see them divided, like portions of a sugary apple tart, into parts which would eventually make up a whole. This is just one more portion of her life she must slot away.

Most days, she is lucky to steal one portion's worth of sewing before somebody comes and touches her busy hands and says,

'Now, Christina, you mustn't worry yourself about that. This is your time to get better.' What she wants to tell them is that she has never once worried about her sewing. She has been a glove maker since the week she turned thirteen, and she misses the long hours sat at her window, her permanently hooked fingers pushing and pulling the plain into the beautiful. This is her creation. She is too proud to beg for it.

'May I close my eyes?' she asks.

The woman, red and round in the face, puffs in response. 'Well, you don't want your eyes to be closed in the photograph, do you?'

'I don't mind.'

The woman puffs again and puts her fists to her significant hips. 'Will it keep you still?'

Christina nods.

'Very well, then.'

There are rows of numbers behind Christina's eyelids: long, tiny, perfectly straight rows, running from one to one hundred. Each number is a stitch, waiting to be crossed off. She strikes a line through each one with her mind, like a shopkeeper checking his stock. Swish. Swish. Swish. When she reaches the fifth and last row, she may pause, but not before; never before. And she cannot move onto a sixth row either, for there is no sixth. She must open her eyes and close them again, to replenish the expended five. These are the rules she has invented, and which she can pretend to adhere to, when she needs to concentrate.

This is not the way she used to create. She used to move her needle to the contours of the glove, sometimes passing whole days without once totalling how many stitches she had made since she woke that morning. Her work had been better then, but her mind had not. Or so she is told. And she suspects – for this is the only logic she can muster on the subject – that perhaps so much unstructured time had allowed it to wander to inappropriate places.

15

'Christina,' the woman says, and Christina opens her eyes. She is a series of zeros this woman – her nose, her eyes, her unnaturally round head. And it is as if she moves around on the inside of one, always on the same circuit, always facing in.

'Yes?'

'Your hands are moving.'

'Does it matter?'

'You know it does. Just as well as you know that you should not be speaking. I'm not fooled by you.'

Christina presses her lips together to keep from smiling, then lays her hands flat on top of the Bible and closes her eyes again. She could count to ten minutes. That might help. She begins tracing the shapes – only her eyes moving, behind the lids – through the straight cut of one, the dips and curves of two, the bulges of three. Ten sets of sixty and she will be allowed to return to her usual routines: to file along a bench and sit to a meal, whether she is hungry or not; to step out into the gardens which front the building as if she is free to leave, only to have to turn and walk back towards the façade she hates because its three floors ought to have five windows each, totalling fifteen, but the doorway reduces the number to fourteen, and she considers fourteen a very nonspecific, come-day-go-day sort of number.

Daniel would be pleased by how precise her thinking has grown. She has not yet fully decided, though, whether she will reveal it to him. If he believes he was right to let the doctor cart her away, well, there is a risk, isn't there, that he might just think to do it again.

'Why am I being photographed?' she asks, pushing the words past the smallest possible parting of her lips.

'For the doctor to measure the difference in you, I would imagine,' the woman says, forgetting her duty for a moment. 'You were photographed when you arrived. Don't you remember?'

'Of course,' Christina says, as though it is a mark of her sanity. But there is no 'of course' about it really. It seems perfectly obvious that lunatics are lunatics on the inside only. Otherwise, why did no one believe her to be one until the Devil spoke her name and she was careless enough to mention it in conversation? She decided weeks ago that the number which best fits lunatics is the eight, for not only is it circuitous, it is also strangled and bursting out of itself. It is, to her eyes, the most uncomfortable of the numbers. To test the theory, she draws its fattened loops in her mind. Then she opens her eyes, just slightly, and lines the image up with the woman standing before her, tilted through ninety degrees, so that she appears to be wearing a pair of spectacles. This Christina finds funny, and begins to laugh.

'What is it now?' the woman asks, and the number-spectacles dissolve and drift away, like a rabble of black butterflies, their wings four delicate sevens tailored neatly together.

'Only that I don't want a photograph of myself,' Christina improvises. 'It's bad enough encountering a mirror, but to be caught forever in this stern pose …'

'Or to be caught forever looking youthful,' the woman suggests, cocking her head to one side and holding a hand up in presentation of her clever perspective. 'I should expect many women would think that a treat.'

'Should you? Then perhaps we might exchange places.'

The woman laughs and Christina finds herself pleased to have caused amusement. It's something she used to do quite a bit of, before she was a lunatic. Perhaps, after all, those scrupulous ten minute portions of this or that have helped a little. She does feel quite ready to return home, to take up her needles and silk and settle in the window seat as she used to; to watch sinister black figures flit under the gas lamps and invent stories for them. Though this is most likely another of the Devil's callings. In fact, it is possible that her stories – naughty stories, of spies and lovers and criminals – had opened Walter up to the Devil in the first place, however much he had enjoyed them.

Still, she hadn't seen any harm in a boy like Walter enjoying what he could. They had always been warned – Christina and her parents – that he would die young.

'Just one more minute,' the woman says, and Christina concentrates on her stillness. Through the slat of her lids she sees the second digits, starting with a broad sixty, parading in reverse order across the large dark square of the camera, like a line of cancan dancers. Fifty-nine, fifty-eight, fifty-seven. The ones with straight legs kick them up nimbly. The eleven is a treat to behold.

'There we are, then,' the woman chirps, though not before Christina has reached zero and begun her countdown afresh. 'All done.'

Christina stands and dips her head from side to side, stretching her neck. The woman – Christina still refuses to call her 'nurse', since she has never once seen the woman administer medicine or tend a wound – directs her to the door, and it is only then that the photographer emerges from under the folds of his dark sheet.

His hair has rubbed against the fabric and strands of it spring free, like curly antennae. He is young and plump-faced. His attire is not as crisp as it might be, but his shoes, Christina notices, are well-shone. It raises her opinion of him.

'Excuse me,' Christina says. The photographer looks lazily in her direction. 'But, how many photographs will there be?'

'How many?' he repeats, though she cannot say why. The question is reasonable enough.

'How many,' she confirms.

'Well, just one, Miss –'

'Mrs Bartlett,' she says. 'Mrs Daniel Bartlett. Just one, you say?'

'Just one, Mrs Bartlett.'

'Very good.'

As she walks back along the corridor towards the larger, noisier part of the building, the woman chattering ahead of her, she allows herself to smile. One. She had hoped he would say one. Nearly a year ago now, she had spent an extremely long, gruelling night teaching herself to find comfort in the straight-backed pride of the number one.

***

The bed next to Christina's is occupied by a Miss Hannah Lyons. The larger portion of her time, Hannah spends lying on her side, her skinny knees raised to her chest, hugging a dirty little doll and singing lullabies to it at a whisper. She does not appear to know how long she has been here, and each time she sees Christina, she asks her the same four questions.

This had unsettled Christina to begin with. She dislikes the four intensely, on account of being so aggressively pointy. Now, she simply chants the same four answers – as she did that first time, to calm the girl – without thinking about the words.

'Who are you?' Hannah asks as Christina reaches the slip of space between their beds. Today, she does not cry or shake, but only flings her eyes from side to side.

'Christina Bartlett,' she answers. 'And you are Hannah Lyons, and we are safe.'

'What about my baby?'

'She is safe, too.'

'Why did they bring me here?'

'Because you refused to let them take your daughter. And it was time to let her go.'

'Then why did they bring you here?'

'Because the Devil visited me, and it was very unfortunate.'

Ordinarily, at this point, Hannah crunches back in on herself and begins muttering her rhymes again. There have been times, though, when Hannah has looked at Christina with eyes so deep with knowledge that Christina has found herself feeling shy, hurt. There is no helping Hannah. She is the number four hundred and forty-four – as sharp and spiky as any person could be.

'Hannah,' Christina says, and it is the first time in a while that she has attempted to engage the girl in real conversation. She believes now that it is all Hannah needs – to be spoken to as though she is normal. Only the in and out of Hannah's breathing is audible, so Christina knows she is listening. 'I'm going home in the morning. I thought you ought to know. Now, I want you to promise me that you will get better, too. Will you promise me that, Hannah?'

Hannah turns slowly over so that she is facing Christina, who is perched now on the edge of her bed. And there is that look. She has understood every word.

'Will you talk about Walter again?' she whispers, and as the room fills with the rasp of hard brushes over floors, and the stewed smell of too many cups of sweet tea, and the rocking of women, and the twitching of women, and – now and then – the screaming of women, Christina describes any detail that comes to mind about her brother. That he was three years younger than she; that he found smiles where others did not; that he patted her head with one big clumsy paw whenever he moved past her; that his ill health left him with a boy's mind and a man's body; that convulsions shook and shook that body until it could shake no longer.

And she is still talking when, eventually, Hannah drops into sleep and all its happy lies.

***

Christina wakes before dawn the next morning. She sits up in bed and makes numbers from the blanketed shapes of the sleeping women. Next to her, Hannah has been transformed from a series of fours into a single tight zero. Beyond her, a pair of slim shoulders and a heavy backside curve into a six. Against the opposite wall, a bunched up eight with a history of violent episodes snores. And next to her, a tall one sleeps stretched out as though she is already in her coffin. This, Christina has found, is the easiest way to think of them – not as names but as figures. Figures who do not have families or pasts. Figures who do not know pain.

The sky fades to grey and the figures rise and stretch or unwrap their hair or, in Hannah's case, resume their singing. And still Christina will not see the people behind the thick black numbers she paints over them. They shift around the room like sums a mathematician cannot take control of, and Christina adds or subtracts them; for fun, yes, but also because she wonders if there is cure to be found in such simple exchanges. If Hannah's grief could be added to Mary's delusion or Carrie's mania, would it be lessened?

Perhaps the doctors have thought of something similar. Perhaps that is why the women are kept in such close quarters. But, musing, Christina decides this doubtful. It seems an altogether too kind and Godly solution for such scientific men to have reached: though perhaps 'Godly' is the wrong thought. God Himself has proven to be something of a disappointment of late. As have a great deal of other men: Walter, who she had trusted to defy the doctors; Daniel, who she had trusted to protect her. It seems to Christina that they all expect more than they are willing to give in return, and, considering the hours and hours she has spent bound over her Bible, she had presumed she would receive better treatment.

Daniel arrives on the dot of nine, and Christina is handed a small case of her own confiscated belongings. She had predicted leaving would take up at least three portions of her day, but the woman who presided over the taking of the photograph simply smiles, releases the case, and waits for her to go – back to her life.

'Is that it?' Christina asks.

The woman, without dropping her smile, nods. 'That's it, Mrs Bartlett. Go home… Oh, wait! I asked the photographer for another of these. I thought your husband might like to keep one.'

Daniel steps forward and retrieves the photograph from the woman's pudgy hand. He smiles down at it. 'It's lovely, Christina.'

'How many of those do you have?' Christina enquires, shortly, and though the woman would usually berate her for using such a tone, today she only looks sympathetic and responds in a charitable way.

'One for the records, Mrs Bartlett,' she answers. Always this 'Mrs Bartlett' now. 'And one for you. Only those two.'

'Two. But he said there would be only one.'

'Who did?' Daniel asks, putting a hand to her shoulder.

'The photographer.'

'Oh, well, does it matter?' He speaks quietly, cautiously. He is trying his best.

'No,' Christina says. 'No, I don't suppose it does… Shall we go?'

'Good luck, Mrs Bartlett,' the woman sings, her zero-shaped face laid open now for Daniel to observe and consider and conclude that she is good. Then, quietly, she adds: 'Perhaps now would be the time to think about children, Christina, if you don't mind my saying so. You're still young enough.' Christina is nearing her twenty-sixth birthday. She no longer feels anywhere close to young. 'Wouldn't that be nice?'

'Yes, I imagine it would,' Christina answers, and she vows silently that if she ever has a child, she will employ Hannah Lyons as her nanny. Only Hannah Lyons.

Daniel smiles and steers her away, the photograph – the second photograph – hanging from his fingers. They ride the train home, cutting through bright green and yellow fields and hardly appearing to advance upon the impossibly distant horizon. They have a compartment to themselves and sit side by side, Daniel cradling Christina's hand between both of his and Christina staring out of the window, studying the changing strokes and circles of light the sun leaves on the glass. She feels as sharp as a seven. She does not try to soften under her husband's touch. She tries instead to find a way to tell him about the numbers. But darkness dribbles down the sky, and they step off the train and walk the lamp-lit streets towards home, and Daniel ushers her through the door, and still she has not spoken. At the sanatorium, she had known that the numbers were indisputable; that they would allow her to communicate safely with her husband. Now, she feels as though they are flowing out from her fingertips like magic spells and abandoning her.

She settles in her window seat and takes her needles and materials from the basket beside it. She measures sheets of black silk with a knowledge which has grown into the bones of her digits, and knows that she holds enough for three fronts or three backs. She sees the threes pressed together, into the shape of a four-leaf clover, and thinks that she could begin by describing this to him – the man who sits across from her, wearing a ring she herself pushed over his slim knuckle. She could tell him that, in the darkness of her dreams, she has rebuilt this room so that it is populated only by numbers: a series of sixes where once there was a wingback chair; a grid of fours, matched tip to tip, where once there was a dark wood cabinet. But she will not utter these words until tomorrow. Today, she is too tired.

'Daniel?'

'Yes.' He watches her with shining eyes, his eyebrows worrying lines into his forehead, and she thinks then that perhaps he does love her after all. Perhaps the Devil got into him for a moment or two as well, that day he allowed the doctor to take her away.

'Would you mind reading to me a while?'

'Not at all. It's been too quiet here without you, Sissy.' And yes, she remembers this. Sissy – the pronunciation Daniel's smallest sister had found in her name. He lowers himself to the floor and kneels before her, his hands looped about her ankles. 'What would you like to hear?'

'Poetry,' she says.

'Do we even have any?'

'Somewhere. There's a Shelley.'

'Well, then. Let's hope it doesn't turn to dust when we open it,' he says and, smiling, he leaves the room to search it out.

Listening to him go, Christina wonders if he remembers the first time he read to her. To keep her eyes from straying towards that part of the room she must avoid, she closes them and replays the memory. It is a memory only of his voice – the first part of him she fell in love with. And his voice is younger than it is now, but she recognises in it the same careful way his tongue orbits his words before releasing them, as light and tender as blown kisses; the same gentle grumbling in his throat which marks the beginning of a new sentence.

He is the same Daniel. She, though, is not quite the same Christina. She is a mathematician now.

Only when she is convinced Daniel is on the opposite side of the house does she chance looking to the spot, in front of the fire, where Walter collapsed that last time. She has spent long months, whilst Hannah nursed her doll, considering the rug he landed on and satisfying herself that, when the time came, she would see there nothing more than lines of burgundy-coloured eights woven into the fabric, enlarged by her imagination to conceal the memory of his splayed body.

It was in that too-slow moment before the convulsing began that the Devil took hold.

'Christina,' he said, just once, and the voice was so different from Walter's own that she knew immediately who was speaking to her. She was angry with God then: not for permitting the Devil to visit her – surely one of His most faithful disciples – but for permitting him to steal Walter's last breaths.

She glares at the rug, trying to force those eights to grow large enough to cover her thoughts. Eights now not because they are the lunatic's number, but because they are endless. Because they do not die; they do not die. But the eights refuse to obey. Christina is struggling, in fact, to decipher the numbers at all. Walter is still there. Walter, shaking and shaking. Walter, finally falling motionless. Walter, his blue eyes wide and hard and suddenly inhuman. And there is no number for that.

'Daniel,' she cries. 'Daniel!'

Above, Daniel's feet thud across on the floorboards as he rushes to answer her call and Christina slumps low in her chair, releasing the silk, which flows away over her knees. Yes, she thinks. He's coming. That's right. There is nothing she wants more now than for Daniel to return, to loop his hands again about her ankles. And when he does, she will not be a hard and lonely seven. She will not be the glove maker, counting out her fears. She will be a bending, pliable nine, and she will curl into her husband and tell him just that – that there is no number big enough to hide her brother's ghost behind. Despite all her efforts, there is no number for that.

Salting Home

In the pale waking hours, the estuary is sprinkled with cockle pickers. From the windows of the cottages which guard the land's tattered edge, they are black dots on a flashing silver mudflat; their Land Rovers are dark squares grumbling against the dawn. At a distance, they are insect-sized and easy to ignore as they bend and straighten, rake and collect. Felicity sits on the exposed rocks below the lighthouse and watches, rubbing the green toes of her wellies together so that they creak.

Today, there are five men. The largest of them tips over his belly to claw his prize from the sand. He is made gnome-like by the waders he wears, the shiny jacket, the woollen hat, his slapped-red cheeks. He rakes and rakes, growing redder each time he bends to touch what he has scraped up, then sieves the young ones away. Though she cannot see them, Felicity imagines the cockles look like little hearts clustered in his palm. Though it is impossible, she pictures them nudging their shells closer together, as if they believe that, by strength of numbers, they might keep their tender bodies safe.

Enzo rushes over the sand nearby, his soft chocolate nose gathering rough grains in layers which he stops to shake off now and then. His paws leave trails of shallow prints, which chase themselves into galaxies. His tail does not stop beating. When he wanders too far away, Felicity calls to him and he comes cantering back, his rump pushed out sideways by his eagerness to please. Sometimes, during these pauses in their morning walk, he sits beside her, looking out over the estuary as if he knows she needs the company: other times, he remembers he is a dog. Felicity had bought Enzo on the first anniversary of her daughter's disappearance, but he's nearly ten now and greying at the muzzle, and she is starting to fear losing him.

She slaps the flat stretch of rock at her side. 'Enzo!' He careers up to her and tumbles onto her lap, too big for it really, his tongue searching the air for her face, his tail drumming her hip. Sand drops from between his pads to work its way into the denim of her jeans and, though it can't have touched her skin yet, Felicity can already feel it itching. She doesn't like loose sand; only the wet, packed-hard kind the cockle pickers feel under their feet. She had passed that aversion on to Jasmine, who, at just three, had winced and stiffened at being set down on the beach. They had come to the lighthouse only in winter after that, when everything was bleached and cold and they could breathe ghosts into the sky.

Felicity sends one from between her lips now, a memory, and wishes it well on its way, as Jasmine used to. She stops just short of waving it goodbye. She began a habit of refusing goodbyes when Aidan threatened to leave. She began a habit, in fact, of refusing everything but this: herself and her dog and that moment when the day breaks open to reveal its naive possibilities.

Aidan does not understand why she cannot abandon her routine now, considering. That's what he says. *Considering*. And Felicity cannot explain it.

She does not want to.

Another hour passes and the cockle pickers stop to drink tea, or coffee, something which steams anyway, from stainless steel flasks which spark against the early sun. It is like watching a clumsy dance routine as they gather together and tilt their hairy chins towards the clouds in tandem. Felicity swallows with them, imagining the hot liquid coursing down into her stomach, making her feel fuller, but she cannot hold the illusion. There is only salt in her mouth.

Her father used to say it was the salt that would bring her home eventually – when she left for university, when she took a research job and stayed away, when she married. 'It's a phenomenon,' he'd say. 'Everyone comes salting home in the end.' And she'd loved that funny phrase, until he had said the same about Jasmine.

'Wherever she is,' he'd insisted, 'she'll come salting home one day.'

Aidan had left the room at those words, silently, loudly, knocking a wedding photo of Felicity's grandparents from the dresser as he went. It would have irritated him for weeks, not stopping to retrieve that photograph, not checking the frame for damage – Felicity knew as much. But he did not stop, and she did not tell him it was undamaged. She hid it in a drawer instead, because those are the games angry people play. And they have played endlessly in the years since, she and Aidan; pretending at illness, pretending at leaving, pretending at beginning affairs. Having them, maybe – Felicity can't be sure.

Now, when she looks at her husband, she sees a man pretending at the man he used to be, a decade ago, and wonders if he encounters the same atrocity in the mirror. She still loves him, though. How that can be true she doesn't know, but she still loves him. She knows because even as she envisages him drowning in the estuary, she does not want to be apart from him. Even as she feels herself drowning, she thrashes her way back. To him.

Enzo's excitement tires him and he settles his head in Felicity's lap, drooling slightly, the wet fur on his legs drying crustily. Felicity turns circles on his skull with her thumb, appreciating the familiar heat he emits.

She had convinced herself that they must not have a dog whilst Jasmine was small. She had convinced herself of a million things that were wrong or did not matter. That, her own mother had told her once, laughing over a spilled bottle of undiluted squash, was motherhood. And Felicity wishes she could locate it again now – that endless happy ache – but she knows it is gone forever.

She is not a mother any more. Someone stole that from her.

The cockle pickers twist the caps back onto their flasks and return to their labour, each man spreading into his own, invisibly-marked patch of sand. The low echoing mutter that was their conversation leaves with the next stroke of wind, and Felicity realises that she has been trying to discern their words all this time, but she has heard none. All the world, it seems, must be kept secret from her now.

A decade ago, she was the secret keeper – protector of her daughter's whispered loves and hopes and worries – and then, overnight, even the newspapers knew more than she did. They knew that Jasmine had blue eyes when Felicity would have sworn they were the gentlest grey; they knew that Jasmine had been tempted through the school gates by a man in a silver Volvo, though Felicity could not believe the same of her clever daughter. Her own mother took to keeping the articles, the paper cut tight to the words by a hand which would not stay steady, then glued into a specially purchased leather diary. And the Family Liaison Officer did her best to convince Felicity that this was fine, that everyone should be allowed to deal with Jasmine's disappearance in their own way, but Felicity didn't buy it. She still doesn't. They should have dealt with it whichever way she had wanted them to.

But she was as good as forgotten in all that grief, Felicity, the onetime mother; just as she has been forgotten in all of this. Because Jasmine is not only her daughter. She is Aidan's too. And she is a granddaughter, and a niece, and a cousin, and a friend.

And she is home, ten years older than any of them have ever known her.

It did not happen as it does in the films. She did not show up on the doorstep, wet through and waiting to be ushered in out of the rain, brought back, as her grandfather had predicted, by the salting in her blood. No instinct called her here. She came by car, escorted by two police officers, a fifteen-year-old girl suddenly who surpasses her mother's height; who narrows her eyes, suspicious always that she is the subject of some elaborate trick; who has breasts and hips and who shares only a slight resemblance with the child Felicity remembers.

This Jasmine does not wear a ponytail which bounces as she skips from room to room. This Jasmine does not sing made-up tunes when she bathes. This Jasmine does not walk on her toes, always teetering towards a future only Felicity has as yet anticipated. She is a stranger who has lived in Felicity's house for just five long days.

The cockle pickers start to move away, turning their backs on Felicity and Enzo – who snores now, his paws twitching through dreams. It is nearly time for the men to leave. Even as they withdraw, though, Felicity concentrates hard on their shrinking outlines. She is afraid to look at the true expanse of empty sand before her, stretching away into open sea. She is afraid it is not empty. When she was five or six, her father told her that horses drown on the estuary: that when the tide is out they roam too far from the shore and can't get back; that their legs stick in the sand and the harder they try to swim to safety, the deeper they sink. Probably, he said it to keep her from venturing out there herself, but she had never doubted the story, and she had always feared seeing a dead horse's head rearing, open-mouthed, desperate, out of the sand. Until Jasmine disappeared. Then her nightmares brought her the image of just one small hand, pale fingers reaching forever for something, anything, solid and finding only water; the unstillable sway of salt water.

Felicity lies back on the rock and lets the cold cradle the back of her skull. There had been an awful sort of reunion when the police left. Her parents had arrived within minutes; Aidan's – having raced dangerously down the motorway – before the morning ticked away. And they'd all sat around then, smiles and tears shining, not knowing what to say but talking constantly, and only Felicity and Jasmine dry-eyed and quiet amongst them. Felicity had tried to exchange a look with the girl – a twist of the mouth which said, *I know, it's horrible isn't it, this, this falsity* – but the girl had not reciprocated.

Really, they have communicated only once. Last night, after Aidan had gone to bed, Felicity had sat in the lounge window, watching the crescent moon fade to nothing. At three, Jasmine had appeared at the bottom of the stairs, still dressed, her eyes dark with lack of sleep. She had opened her mouth, then changed her mind and shrugged, and Felicity had done nothing more than shrug back, because she understood that there were no words which could help them overcome this. They did not know each other, these two. They no longer shared those tiny, curious things which made them mother and daughter. It had been too long. They would both remain lost forever.

Felicity had gone to bed soon after, and opened her window and hung out, dragging the sharp, close smell of the sea into her body until she shuddered with it. Until her every muscle trembled. She was waiting – she knew even then, though she would admit it, will admit it, to no one – for the sound of wood meeting wood, for the sound of a door closing.

She wakes to find the cockle pickers packing their Land Rovers, throwing their rakes and plunders inside, laughing out their goodbyes. The slamming doors punch holes in the quiet. Above, the seagulls circle, riding a roundabout, shrieking for scraps. It was perhaps just half an hour, but it is the first time she's slept in days.

Enzo resumes his explorations as though his nose has not already marked this exact path tenfold. Then one of the cockle pickers whistles for his friend's attention, Enzo's ears perk up, his tail stops wagging, and he is still for less than a second before he takes off, his body tucking and releasing as if he is being catapulted unwillingly into every forward bound. Felicity starts immediately after him, legs heavy as her wellies are sucked into the sand, but of course she makes no advance on the dog. He is a rocket, skimming the sand. He is headed straight for the cockle pickers. And Felicity is too embarrassed – her legs buckling, her breath heaving, her chest bouncing – to shout after him, so she just keeps running, a mad woman sprinting dangerously towards five men, afraid suddenly that this will become some sort of incident; that one of them will kick Enzo and injure him; that, for the first time in his life, Enzo will bite someone; that a chance encounter will culminate in a lengthy court case and a final trip to the vet. Felicity is full of old, stupid fears. And she is full of them not because Enzo is misbehaving, but because when Jasmine stepped down the stairs last night she was carrying a bag. She was carrying a heavy bag. And Felicity had not asked her to put it down.

Noticing Enzo's approach, one of the cockle pickers drops onto his haunches to catch the dog, and, easily captured, Enzo throws himself onto his back to have his ribs scrubbed by a large, sand-worn hand.

'I'm sorry,' Felicity calls as she nears. 'I'm so sorry.'

'Don't worry.' The cockler smiles down at Enzo, charmed. But Felicity cannot calm herself now. Tears clog her throat.

'I'm so sorry,' she says as she cries and smiles and cries, because, yes, she is sure she heard the back door open and close last night, she is sure, and the relief of it is sweet enough to make her sob, and she's sorry for that, she's sorry, but her daughter has been dead for ten years, and you can't, you can't, you just can't come salting home a decade after you've been mourned.

The cockle pickers are kind to Felicity. They offer her tea from their flasks and fuss over the dog and wait for her tears to stop. By the time they start their engines and rumble back to shore, the estuary is slick with returning water. Their tyres flick salty beads up behind them as they depart: it looks, Felicity thinks, like they are churning up rows of pearls. Climbing back over the rocks towards the lighthouse, she stops to watch them drive out of sight, the diminishing jolt and sway of them. And she wonders, as they go, how many cockles are chattering against each other in the bumping Land Rovers' boots, and how many are still nestled in the sand, still lost, growing safer with each deepening inch of incoming water.

Bullet Catch

Dahl's newest stage show spectacular!
A work of powerful magic and boundless imagination.

They spent long, precise days rigging the gun up correctly. At intervals, Victor sneaked in and watched from behind the white gauze fabric of the wood-framed screens as Bill and Edgar fired and fired at the same hole, sending paint fragments ricocheting around the narrow space. After each shot, they measured to see if the target was widening, made some small adjustment, then began again. Pop, pop, pop. And almost every time they nodded as they released the measuring tape and let it unroll, like a black and white tongue, to the floor. But even when they didn't, Victor knew they were dealing in fractions of nothing. To his eye, the hole did not appear to change, and that was good enough for him.

After all, it was he who had persuaded them that it could work; he who had gathered the team, laid out the procedures.

'People have been pretending at this for hundreds of years,' he'd said. 'We're going to do it properly. The genuine way.'

He'd explained it all to Florence one lazy morning. How even into this century the Bullet Catch had been a cheap trick – dummy guns, blanks. How, when the audiences had demanded it, performers had started risking the real thing. And how they'd died; so many of them had died. He and Florence had been in bed for three or four days, watching time turn through a pair of thin cotton curtains: the sun spraying the room gold; the rain

34

scattering bubbles of light across the plaster-white walls. Outside the window, Vienna bustled on without them.

'There's no way you can attempt it and know you'll be safe,' Florence said. 'I don't believe there is.'

'Ma Sul Lee has done it five times in the last eight years,' Victor answered, blowing a few stray strands of her hair off his chest.

Ma Sul Lee was his hero. Nearly ninety years of age and the old Korean was still spitting hot bullets from between his teeth. He was the master of the Bullet Catch, and for a long time Victor had hoped he would be able to train under him. That was why he'd followed him to Vienna. However successful Victor's shows became, though, Lee still refused to take him on as his apprentice; refused, in fact, to take any apprentice at all. All of Vienna was worried now that he would die without sharing his secret. He was the only man, after all, to survive the genuine Bullet Catch.

Victor did not tell Florence that. He said the same thing to her – when he first voiced his plans, high on hours of tasting her freckled skin – as he later said to his assistants. 'Ma Sul Lee might have been lucky once, but no one falls lucky nine straight times. It has to be down to technique.'

Now, as Victor stood before the blasted wall, the cup clamped between his shielded teeth, he couldn't quite believe they had trusted his words. Whatever Lee's secret was no one had yet managed to expose it.

Dahl wows audience with vanishing act!
Girl retrieved from Vienna Zoo hours later. Dahl promises more!

The gun was bolted in place, near the top of its metal pyramid. The screens were angled so that he could see no one but his shooter, Gina. In the spaces between the screens, though, Victor could make out the shadows of Bill and Edgar and Florence, stretched long. Occasionally, Bill and Edgar lowered their heads together to whisper something he could not hear, but he was trying not to worry. Their job was to keep him safe. He had to trust them to it. He concentrated instead on staring into Gina's wide glassy eyes, and hoped none of them could see the glob of saliva that was rolling from the left corner of his mouth. He wanted to adjust the cup, but it was too late now.

As the weeks had passed and Florence had realised he really was going ahead with it, she had tried to talk Victor out of attempting the Bullet Catch.

'You're just trying to get his attention,' she said. 'You're being reckless.'

Victor grasped her hand. They were walking past the Staatsoper building as night swirled over Vienna, lacing strips of scarlet and lavender into the pearly clouds. The ancient stone was the colour of candlelight in the city dusk. He pulled her under one of the open archways.

'You don't need to be anyone's apprentice,' she went on. 'The whole city knows who Victor Dahl is.'

Victor shook his head. 'I don't want the whole city to know. I want the whole world to know.'

Florence smiled and lifted her hands to curl her hair into a ball and release it again: it unwound down her back, the colour of long-fallen leaves. She always did that when she was lost for words, Victor had noticed. And he had been surprised by the noticing. He had never known so much about a woman as he did about Florence. At twenty-three, she was six years his junior, and when they'd met, he hadn't expected for one minute that she would be able to hold him as she did; that she would be able to drop ideas into his mind which stuck there.

'I suppose,' she said, 'the whole world knows who Ma Sul Lee is.'

He leaned in to kiss her then, but just as he got close enough to feel her breath on his lips, there came a cracking of wings and a clutch of pigeons shot into the air like fired grey arrows. Florence ducked out from under the archways to watch them, dragging Victor with her. But Victor did not see them. He was watching her: the flickering of her eyelashes as she followed their flight; the parting of her petal-lips as she tipped back her head.

'Are you ready?' Gina asked now. Victor stared far into her eyes, trying to find the exact points of her pupils. From this distance, he couldn't distinguish them. Why should he be able to? He didn't know those eyes at all. He had never considered their gold-splashed irises as he leaned in for a kiss, or waited for them to open onto the morning, or observed them made larger by gathering tears.

'No,' he said, spitting the cup into his hand. 'No.' You had to have complete faith in your shooter. You had to hand them control. And there had been stories, in some cases, of shooters deliberately misfiring, sending the bullet into a shoulder or a stomach or square between the eyes. Gina's eyes were unblinking and suddenly severe. She released the gun and stood upright, scowling.

'I want Florence to do it,' he said.

Gina snorted. Then, understanding slowly that he meant it, she put her hands to her angular hips and began to pace back and forth. '*Florence* is not a shooter,' she said through stiff lips. 'If *Florence* decides to hesitate or cry or… faint, you know what'll happen.'

'Still.'

'But this is just the run-through. We can do some work with her before the show, if that's what you want – *her* up on stage with you. She can practise.'

Perhaps it was fear that had made him say it – so that there would be a delay, an argument, a postponement even. But now that he had said it, it made perfect sense. Florence would pull the trigger; now, and when he did it onstage. It would work. They knew each other. And by the end of the year, he would aim to rival Lee's nine-time record. There would be no mysterious months-long absences from Victor Dahl. He would attempt the Bullet Catch every few weeks; every time he stepped into the stale air of a new theatre. By the end of the year, he would set a record of his own. Florence had voiced her doubts, certainly, but she'd encouraged him too. 'Yes,' she'd said when he told her about Lee or explained what he was planning for his new show. 'Yes. You can do anything.' And Victor had believed her.

He had to believe in something, when he was standing in front of a loaded gun.

Victor of Vienna in death-defying act!
Beautiful assistant becomes city's darling.

Florence stepped sideways through the gap between the screens, twisting the ends of her hair around one circling finger.

'Can you do it?' he asked.

Florence shook her head gently. Or he thought she did. Florence always was so difficult to decipher: whenever he upset her, or pleased her, or frightened her, she would halt him with the same arcane stare. She was doing it now, looking up at him from beneath her brows, biting at her bottom lip. Victor could just see the place where two of her teeth overlapped.

'You can,' he said.

Florence breathed deep and, without saying a word, slinked towards the gun. Victor had not realised how small, how tight and unsparing her body was until now, when she and Gina stepped around each other, careful to avoid contact, as though they were engaged in a formal dance. In comparison, Gina looked strong, reliable, sturdy.

Florence turned to him again, awaited his nod of encouragement, then took one final step onto the shooting mark.

There was a beauty to it all now, Victor thought: the exact swing of her hips when she moved; the dim, screened lamps; the shadows which stretched to forever. It was all running in slow motion. Florence took a long while positioning herself, sliding her feet further and further apart as she brought her hand up to the trigger and settled her elbow on the pyramid. When she was comfortable, she looked to Victor and winked, slow and serious, the black curves of her lashes stencilled onto her cheeks by the leaking lamplight, and Victor was reminded, in some small way, of his mother.

It was not the way she looked. Leona Dahl had been as gypsy-dark as her son. It was the wink. His mother used to wink at him like that: as if she knew something he didn't; as if he was being humoured. Left backstage at one of her shows, Victor would sulk about it for hours.

He turned the cup in his hand. 'Why did you wink?'

Florence peered over the top of the gun. 'I was trying to make you relax,' she said. Her face was flat and worried. In this light, Victor noticed, the freckles on her cheeks were lost. She looked like a mannequin.

'Alright.' Victor lifted the cup.

'You're not,' she said. 'You're not sure, are you? We shouldn't do it if you don't trust me.'

'I'm sure,' Victor replied. 'Honestly. On the count of three.' He swallowed all the saliva he could and pushed the metal cup back between his teeth. It didn't feel right. It pressed a bitter taste onto his tongue and he tried to remember what Florence tasted like, to lessen it, but the sensation was gone. Still, there was no turning back now. It was just one shot. Just one bullet. Just one catch.

He held his right hand in a fist, slightly away from his body, and uncurled his index finger, as he and Gina had planned. That was the count of one. And with it came the ability, suddenly, for Victor to feel every drop of his blood, surging around his body.

His hand throbbed; his head pounded, louder than any gunshot; his heart shrunk into a prune. He uncurled a second finger. Florence was right, he wasn't sure, but he was willing to risk it. He closed his eyes and thought back to the beginning of his training; the little tricks the stagehand had shown him while he waited in the dressing rooms for Leona to finish her performances. He'd known about Ma Sul Lee even then. He'd decided, when his legs still swung in the space between chair and floor, where he was going, what he would become. He wouldn't let anything distract him now. Not doubt or fear. Not even Florence. Because Florence might disappear as abruptly as she had appeared, as abruptly as his mother had, but fame… Even if it faded, it would endure somewhere – on a yellowing sheet of newspaper, or on a poster, or in a memory.

Spectators fight for tickets as
brave Florence resumes city's most spectacular show.

He opened his eyes and uncurled his third finger in one swift movement. Yes, he thought, he was willing to risk everything, everything, so that the world would know his name. The newspapers would write headlines about him then, and theatre-goers would raise their just-filled glasses to a night to top all nights, and children in Vienna and Berlin and Paris and London would bend over their toy magic boxes and – he had just enough time, before Florence pressed the trigger, to send her a wink back – Victor Dahl, they would say. I want to be like Victor Dahl.

The Dog Track

The dogs spring open and snap shut like hinged puppets as they hurtle round the track, chasing the white rabbits of they own freezing breaths. Above, the sky is black as nightmares. The men at the trackside, they roar so loud it grows distant-like, muted, and I listen for the rushing sound that must be coming from them galloping dogs, but I can't find it. My ears is too full. Perhaps this is what drowning feels like.

I told them, at the hospital, that he likes coming to the dogs. He might do. I don't know. I did find the ticket crumpled in his coat pocket and, when I straightened it out, saw them words, looking like undiscovered hieroglyphs they'd been rubbed so much.

That's why I've come – to find if there's anything worth discovering. And to pretend: to say to strangers, 'my husband's usually here himself but he's unwell,' and see if they believe me.

So far, I haven't found anyone to talk to. They're a cleft-faced lot at the track; the skin on they cheeks and foreheads cracked in the shapes of so much disappointment. Here, they betting on a way out.

The dogs shoot past like a cluster of comets and I lean forward over the rail, watching they arched bodies pull tight, then stretch out, burning; watching them tails of sand they kick up. I've chose trap six, but I can't see him from here. Under the thousand-watt bulbs, only they spines is visible; the curved white lines like nails on the end of ten fingers. Or like they bone's showing through they thin, flat hair.

I want to shout with them punters, so I open my mouth and go, 'Six! Six!'

There's no need to find better words. No one's listening.

I chose trap six 'cause he was the saddest looking. 'Cause his brindle coat hung too slack over his knuckly muscles. 'Cause he reminded me of my brother. He comes in second-to-last, and they laugh, them men next to me, maybe 'cause they won, so I decide to stay and put more on him next time. Poor Night Runner. He's in need of encouraging.

It might be I'm expected back at the hospital. I don't know. Or I do know, and the chemical-like smell draped across my inside-face is making me ignore that I know. Beside, I'm unfamiliar now with being tied to a person. Visiting is seven till eight, so I've missed my slot – though I s'pose that doesn't apply to me, now I'm a wife with a comatose for a husband. I haven't asked and no one's thought to tell.

But then, I haven't told, either. Not what they need to hear.

My dog goes again at nine. The traps bangs open, he lurches out, his claws scrabble for something solid in the sand and, when he gets his good rhythm going, he's already behind, hunting the vanishing smell of them others. His start's poor. That speed of his is decent-like, though. I scream shapeless sounds at him when he catches, then passes the trailing dog and joins they pack. His pink-curl tongue drops out from between his teeth, heavy like an anchor that keeps him in his position. He's happy, letting them other animals take they lead.

I poke my own tongue out, to find what the cold tastes of, then suck it back in again when my s'liva fizzes like lemon sherbet.

When I got to the hospital, I tried to look frenzied-like, like them dogs do. I unbrushed my hair with my hands and went just as I was, like a real wife would. 'I had a phone call,' I said, but I couldn't be no more intimate than that. I couldn't say 'about my husband' like I was s'posed to. I couldn't claim him.

My dog lopes in fourth. Not bad. The man, him standing next to me, he scrunches his ticket in an angry fist and throws it onto the track. It doesn't travel far. It catches the churning cold current and spins downward, slow, like a jagged snowflake.

They didn't ask me to prove who I was at the hospital. Didn't ask for no marriage certificate, or for me to stand between two nurses and point out the right blanket-rolled body. They just dialled my phone and I said 'hello', and they said my name, and I said 'hello' again, and then they gave me a husband. Though, asking shocked wives for evidence of this or that ain't a matter for nurses, I don't s'pose. Quite right-like. Anyway, who'd claim a man stupid or unfortunate enough to drive himself under a train if that man weren't truly they own?

I could have told them they was wrong on the phone. That's my name, I could've said, but I haven't got any husband. Even later I could've said it, whilst they was ushering me about with soft looks and kind words. Anything would have been better than opening my own hands up to this decision I'm carrying about like some mind-boulder. On or off? I could've avoided it, 'cept something dragged me along with they mistake – that same thing, maybe, that crouches in your gut and makes you want to do things like look up at the moon or walk in that same direction a river flows.

I check the boards. Night Runner has one more race to go. A fluid-like sort of ache starts in my stomach and I recognise it, 'ventually, as pity. I did not pity the comatose man. I won't admit that to no one, though, 'cause it might mean I'm the worst kind of person. But then, I don't s'pose the worst kind of people know that about themselves – that that's what they are.

I hand a fifty-note to the bookie. I say, 'Night Runner, please. To win.'

And when the bookie slides the note into his pocket, he's smirking, thinking he's had the better of me. I smirk back, 'cause that's the defence I learned as a kid. I used it on my brother till it nearly drove him mad.

That's how it went when we were tiny. Him always teasing, looking for reactions – from me; from anyone. Then, when he got none, hurling tantrums round the room like as if they was poison in his blood. He'd kick and scream and rage until it all leaked out of him, then he'd drop asleep, and I'd carry him to his bed – at least, when he was still little enough to coil himself up like a seashell I would.

He was a storm, my brother; the eye and the messy aftermath.

When nine-thirty comes, Night Runner's pushed into his trap for the last time. To my both sides, loose ropes of men stand and inspect they tickets. They is middle-aged-like mostly: bald or balding; made even stouter than reality by they fat coats. Under the floodlights, they as pale as stars.

'Anyone taking they chance on Night Runner?' I ask. Them rope of men, knotted together with disgust at my stupid question, glare at me and I smirk. Sometimes, I set up these exchanges. Sometimes, I remember my brother this way.

The traps make they metallic clang and the dogs are launched, or scared, into they race. Night Runner makes his same bad start. He's last leaving the traps, legs tight, ears flat-like. The pack begins to move away and pity gurgles up in my stomach. I know how it feels, being left behind. My brother did it to me when he died.

As they reach the first corner, Night Runner, he's opening out, gaining, and I scream him on till my throat rattles. The man next to me, he takes a step away and I laugh. It's hard to care what another person thinks when you got life in your palms, and I want to tell him this, but the secret's too good-like for sharing. On or off? One small word or another. That's all they want from me, the accidental wife. The doctor, when he swept in to talk abstractions, he left me with only one real message: whatever I decide, the comatose man, he won't recover to be himself again. So I don't know what it is I'm choosing for him, really.

Perhaps all I have power enough to offer is darkness or deeper darkness.

Night Runner takes the final corner outside of the pack. He's moving okay-like. But when they straighten up for the rush to the line, this smaller, nimbler dog slips by and breaks his tempo. Night Runner stumbles sideways, tired.

'Your punt's going to stagger in last,' the man nearby me warns. He's been shoved close again by the crowd.

'I know,' I say. 'That's why I backed him.'

The man elbow-nudges his friend, rolling his runny eyes. 'Are you listening to this?' he says. 'She's gone soft!'

Despite his stumble, Night Runner crosses the line barely a breath behind them other racers, and I decide not to argue with the man. Instead, I watch who'll collect the dog and, when I spot this scrawny chap – fag-smoke rising behind his glasses to hide his eyes – leaning over the railings and hooking on a lead, I shove my way through the milling punters after him.

At the car park, I lose sight. Black-jacketed, he's just another wrong-angled shadow, and that panics me a bit 'cause I can't see his face, and that's always panicked me: since my brother died, anyway, and there was only me, fifteen and sad and not sharing home with my ferocious, thirteen-years-old protector any more. We divided that role between us – protector and protected – depending how bad-like our father's day went.

I find Night Runner's owner again when he pushes his key into his car door and it makes that funny click-noise they make. I'm close enough to see him swipe a sideways kick at the dog. And before I can even shout at that scrawny chap, I'm running at him; I'm thrown forward, like waves at a cliff face, by my anger-instinct; I am loud-like on the inside and silent on the outside. I am a storm.

And I'm all these things because the dog didn't flinch at the kick. That's why I'm storming for him – why I must. 'Cause he did not flinch.

The scrawny chap's arms, they go up when he sees, peripherally, my fuming self tearing toward him. He frees Night Runner's lead and the dog, he makes the jump he was punished for hesitating over. The chap wraps his head up in his hands, cowers a bit, and then I hit him, hard-like, with all my moving weight, and he sprawls into the gravel and it makes the sound like coins cascading from a slot machine.

'I'll give you all I've got for the dog,' I say. The cash came from the comatose man's pocket. I didn't struggle claiming that.

I expect the scrawny chap to be outraged. At the least to start haggling, alleging his dog worth this and his dog did that. But he makes no exaggerations.

'How much do you have?' he asks.

'Hundred,' I answer, and even before my mouth closes, I wish I'd said 'a ton' and sounded like I cared less.

'Take him,' the chap says, rocking himself up into a sitting position. 'You can take him for that.'

I count out the notes, stack them on the car-top, lean in, retrieve the dog, and start backing away. As we go, I murmur to Night Runner, in case he's afraid. There's nothing worse than silence, when you're afraid. And perhaps that's what I'll do for the comatose man, too – alleviate his silence. He might be frightened. Frightened as Night Runner. Frightened as me.

'Come on then, boy,' I say, my voice smooth as the best dreams. 'We've got things to do, you and me. We've got truths to tell…'

I can't call him Night Runner. That's no proper name.

'How about… Gunner?' I say. 'Will you answer to that?' At my side, the dog walk on, head low, not caring to listen. 'How about we try it?' I coax. 'If you don't like it, we can find you something else, something opposite.' But sometimes, the smallest changes are what's needed. Like standing up when a drunk leans into your face, breathing three per cent insults. Like betting on a dog though you know he's about to lose. Like filling a comatose man's timeless hours with poetry or music 'stead of nurses' chatter – that's a small change, but it could be the biggest too.

We reach the place where the car park straggles into taloned weeds and then fields deep with thick, swishing grass. I stroke Gunner's shingly skull, working the hair the right way so it lays flat and elegant. He's as elegant as any creature could be, my Gunner. He's a blue sky, not a storm.

I unclip his lead. 'Run if you want, boy,' I whisper. In front of us there's a world's worth of questions, hiding in the waist-deep grass, burrowing under the cold-packed earth.

'Run,' I say, 'but only if you want.'

Her Last Show

'This is the one my darlings,' she says, twirling around in the middle of the empty room. She holds her right hand out to her side, bent at the elbow and wrist, her thumb and forefinger pinched as though she is hanging an ornament on a Christmas tree. It's a pose her mother taught her, but she forgot the learning of it years ago. It is as natural to her now as this moving from place to place. It's the life.

The children stand in the doorway, each holding a small, faded suitcase. Evelyn gets a flash of them each time she turns, as though she is seeing a film from thirty years ago – its reel stuttering frantically but the characters hardly moving. She pauses, raises her eyebrows.

'Come and spin with your mother,' she demands, 'or I shan't be happy.'

Neither of them moves. Rosa glares at Evelyn, her dark eyes dull and unblinking. At her side, Mickey looks down at the floor, chewing his lip. Where they hold hands, Rosa's knuckles are pointed and white.

Evelyn throws back her head and clutches at her chest. 'Oh,' she cries. 'I shall never be happy again if my children refuse to play with me.' She lifts her head just long enough to peek at them. Mickey takes a step towards her, but he is stopped by Rosa's stubborn grip and he springs back towards his sister like a dog on a tightened chain.

'Oh,' Evelyn cries again, dropping to her knees. One of her kneecaps makes a crunching sound when it hits the floorboards, but she ignores the jolt of pain which scatters up her leg. 'I can feel my heart breaking,' she says. 'It's going to crack into tiny pieces. You're going to have to sweep it all up and stick it back together again.'

Mickey begins to smile and strains against Rosa's grip once more, and this time she lets him go. His suitcase thuds to the floor and tips onto its side, and Evelyn notices that the lock is broken – he must have been holding it shut all day. As he approaches, she tries to jump to her feet, but her shoe snags in the hem of her dress and Mickey has to put his hands out to help her. She clasps them, stands, and shapes a wide smile for him before they start to spin. This is their favourite game, and soon, their feet sound like galloping hooves on the bare floor. They tip their heads back as they move faster and faster. Evelyn notices a dusty chandelier dangling from the centre of the ceiling, its base a confusion of carved white mermaids.

'Look, Rosa,' she calls. 'Come and look at this.' She does not check to see if Rosa is watching. She can't bear to see the girl look at her as her father did, in the end, those dark eyes made darker still by her reflection in them. But something persuades Rosa to join in, and when she steps across the floorboards towards them, Evelyn and Mickey part hands to let her slip into the circle. It is only then that Mickey laughs. The sound makes Evelyn want to curl into her bed and weep. But, she remembers, she has no bed of her own here yet.

They spin too fast for their mismatched strides and they stumble, gripping each other's hands for support. Finally, Rosa laughs too, the strange sound hooting out suddenly from such a shocked face that she appears, Evelyn thinks, to be remembering an ability she had lost. The hoots make them giggle all the more and, as they grow weaker, they crumple, one after another, onto the floor. They lie back and stare up at the ceiling, and Evelyn steals the opportunity to pull her children to her. Together, they drift into silence. Slabs of sunlight thrust through the windows, exposing the atlas long-neglected damp has painted across the walls, and Evelyn attempts to sigh away the little dots of dust which are threatening, already, to settle over them. She attempts to make them dance.

'We'll be back on track after this one,' she says quietly. 'This will be the last move, alright? Alright?' She feels Mickey nodding his head, his hair brushing against her chest.

For a moment, Rosa is still. Then, without saying a word, she stands and walks away, her footsteps echoing off those fissured walls.

Evelyn sits up to watch her disappear through a doorway, her yellow dress swinging behind her, then flattens herself back to the floor and hugs Mickey hard. Squeezing her eyes shut, she begins humming a made-up tune. She doesn't want to think about Rosa, standing stiff in the middle of another empty room, crying into the back of her hand so that her sobs don't make a sound.

As she cuts Mickey's sandwiches for school the following day, Rosa listens to the rain hitting the windows. It sounds sharp, like a pecking bird, and when it runs down the glass it glints with a hundred different colours. In the darkness beyond, London is vast and full and empty all at the same time. Earlier, she had stood and looked for the details, but all she could make out were blurs of indigo and ruby and gold on a thick black backdrop.

Somewhere, her mother is standing onstage.

She slides the sandwiches into Mickey's bag, next to his books, and goes back to the window. She is half-reflected back at herself. The slash of red lipstick she put on hours before is as ugly on her soft face now as it was then, and she wishes again that she had her mother's angular features, that her cheekbones sliced across her face in that same starved way.

She would put beauty to much better use than her mother ever had. She would use it to hurt people, not to make them love her.

Rosa knows the show hasn't been going well – she's checked the papers. One week into a four week run and there have been complaints. Evelyn has been missing her cues; people have been walking out; there's been talk she's been fall-about drunk before curtain up. Whether she's drunk before the show starts or not, though, she is certainly drunk by the time she gets home. Rosa lies in bed and listens to her clattering in at three, four o'clock. Most of the time, Raymond comes with her. But something has changed. Evelyn had always managed the drink before, sipping her way through two or three splashes of whiskey and staying cheerful. Lately, it turns her pale.

Rosa goes to Mickey's bedroom, to put her ear to the gap between door and frame he insists on and check he is asleep. They have a bedroom each here; three big, white rooms with nothing inside them but the mattresses the last owners left behind. Evelyn had brought less with them each time they moved. But the place looks grand from the outside: the red bricks, the stucco mouldings, the oak double-doors that lead in off the pavement. And that's the important part. Evelyn Dean has a reputation to uphold.

Rosa knows what people imagine – cocktail parties and suited staff and red-lipped laughter. It had been that way once. But now … tonight she had picked blue spots from the bread before she'd buttered Mickey's sandwiches.

There is no movement inside his bedroom. She pulls the door tight shut and twists the handle to make sure it doesn't drift open. She is waiting for the doorbell to ring, and she doesn't want him to hear anything.

She doesn't know yet how loud it will be.

That they had moved into the new apartment the same day the show started was no accident. Raymond had arranged it that way. It was his way of persuading her to go on. Evelyn glances towards the place, just offstage, where he always stands. He is mostly in shadow, but she can still make out the hard line of his jaw and, despite herself, she imagines running her tongue along it. She understands now that he manipulates her. But she understands, too, that it is for her own good.

'We weren't ready,' she'd said to him in the quiet after opening night. They were rolled up in bed. 'I told you we weren't ready and you promised me it would be good.'

'It's publicity, Eve,' he'd explained. 'What does it matter if it's good or bad? Your name will be back in the papers.'

When she'd argued that her name had never left the papers, he'd scoffed then pulled her against him and pressed his teeth into her shoulder. Later, she'd found the two perfect curves in the mirror, printed pale green on her skin. No one had told her that the papers had stopped running stories about her.

A man in the pit shouts something. Evelyn doesn't know what. It reaches her as a guttural clump of sound. But she's used to this now: to standing and being shouted at; to being hated. She's afraid it will happen with Ray, too, eventually. She'd noticed the way he'd looked at Rosa last week – a smirk interrupting a tender frown – and that night, in bed, Evelyn had giggled like a schoolgirl. If he wanted a fifteen-year-old, she could be one. She could be anything he needed. She'd been doing it her whole life.

By the time the show finishes, half of the audience have gone. Evelyn had watched them shaking their heads and tutting as they walked out. 'Darlings,' she called after them. 'Are you really turning your backs on Evelyn Dean? I've not been feeling well, my darlings. Not well at all. Please stay.' But they hadn't. They hadn't even looked back, and Evelyn had gone on with her next song as the doors swung closed behind them.

Now, she takes a long curtsey and waits for her applause. It comes in little patches, as inconsistent as incoming fog, and she staggers offstage to escape it. That pain at her core is back and she needs to sit down.

'How was I, Ray?' She waves her hand at him, so he can take it and kiss her knuckles, as he always has, but his arms stay crossed at his chest. Evelyn flicks her hair over her shoulder and performs a little wiggle: she developed the move just after *Shirley*, when she'd had to manage the transition to older roles, and it has worked beautifully over the years. 'I thought it went very well. That top note was a sensation. Did you hear it, Ray?'

'It was a mess.' He turns to walk away.

Evelyn shuffles after him and, reaching out, manages to graze his back with her fingernails before a new dizziness stops her. 'No, Ray. No,' she calls after him. 'It wasn't so bad, my angel. There were moments of, well, greatness. The old greatness! It was just like when I was Shirley –'

Her words make Ray stop, too. He spins around, grips her arms. 'You're not Shirley anymore, you stupid woman. Look at you. You were Shirley for five minutes, thirty years ago. You've been a joke ever since.'

'Don't say that.' Evelyn shakes her head. 'I shan't forgive you if you say such a thing again.'

He rubs a hand across his forehead. 'Yes,' he mumbles. 'You will.'

Pulling one arm free, Evelyn raises her hand and slaps him, as hard as she can. His head snaps sideways. The crack of it echoes around the theatre. When he looks back at her, there is a bright bump where one of her rings has caught the curve of his eye socket. He blinks the sting away then drags her towards him. 'I'm sorry,' she murmurs into his chest. 'I'm sorrier than I've ever been in my whole long life.' She nuzzles the loose fabric at the neck of his shirt until her nose finds skin: he smells of smoke and sweet drink and, somewhere beneath that, soap.

'I just want you to do well,' Ray says. 'Remember how it used to be, when we were doing well? We used to have fun, didn't we?' He strokes her hair with one hand and holds her to him with the other. Her tears are hot. They run down his chest and soak into the thin cotton of his shirt, leaving marks like grease spatter.

'Do you wish I were younger, Ray?'

'Of course not.'

They are standing between two tall set pieces – the backgrounds to something. Large black boxes sit here and there. Coils of electrical wire unwind slowly on the floor. Evelyn doesn't remember theatres looking this way. She remembers being escorted offstage and straight into a bar or outside to meet the press, not this miserable place. 'I saw you looking at Rosa,' she says. 'I don't blame you. She's a pretty girl, my pretty girl … she could be a star, don't you think?'

Ray puts his hands to her face and tilts her head up, bringing them eye to eye. 'I wasn't looking at Rosa,' he says. 'She asked me to help her, that's all.'

'To get into the business? Will you?'

Ray takes a long time to answer. Evelyn notices that, though his face is calm now, it is flat and tight and strange to her. There is a visible pulse beneath his ear, beating like a heart.

'No,' Ray says. 'She's too young… next time she asks, I'll tell her no.'

Rosa opens the door before his finger has released the bell. She's been waiting behind it, her eye to the peephole. He is wearing a long coat and hat, and he smiles at her without speaking. He looks older than she had imagined he would: his beard is thick as creeping moss, and when he stops smiling the wrinkles around his eyes fail to unfold. She stands aside and opens the door properly, so that he can step in.

'Are we on our own?' he asks.

Rosa nods her head then touches a fingertip to the corner of her mouth to make sure she has not smudged her lipstick. She is wearing one of her mother's silk nightgowns, the arms falling inches over her hands. Her stomach is making empty sounds which she hopes he cannot hear. She put what was left of the jam in Mickey's sandwiches; there was nothing else in the cupboards.

The man scans the room for somewhere to sit. Finding nowhere, he removes his coat and drapes it over the kitchen counter. He places his hat on top of it and the money on top of that. As he moves around the apartment, Rosa considers how tall he is, how strong his arms look. He reminds her a little of Ray, and she wonders if they are more than friends – if, perhaps, they're somehow related – but she doesn't ask. She'd begged Ray to help her with this, and she's afraid now that she will say something to ruin it. She's afraid, too, that she will not ruin it.

He loosens his tie, hooks it up over his head and lets it fall. It curls onto the floorboards like a serpent. 'In here?' he asks.

Rosa shakes her head, forces herself to stand a little straighter. She's ready. She has to be. 'In there,' she says and moving towards him, she takes his hand. His skin feels as rough against hers as the branches of the trees she'd climbed last week with Mickey.

No one calls an end to the show. Night after night they watch her stumble onstage: the audiences dwindle; the performances get worse. But she is Evelyn Dean. She played Shirley once. No one thinks they have the right to tell her she's a disaster. They're waiting for her to realise it herself.

Evelyn spends more and more time in bed. Whenever she is not onstage, she lies and drinks a watery mixture of whiskey and her own tears. It's the only thing, she says, that stops her feeling so cold. She keeps the room dark, and winces when Rosa opens the door to bring in her lunch. There are moments, though, when she sees her children and remembers that she ought to be a mother. Then, she encourages them to jump on the bed, or asks Mickey to tap dance or sing while she and Rosa sit tucked under her sheets and cheer. Then, she thinks she is doing a good job.

'Rosa, darling,' she calls now, 'can you get your old mother her medicine? I'm so cold, Rosa. So cold.'

'There's none left,' Rosa calls back. The medicine is a simple cough mixture which Rosa takes the label off. It does nothing.

'Then go and buy some, sweetheart.'

Standing at the window, Rosa shoves her hand in her pocket to count the coins there. Most of what she earned last week is gone, spent on food and whiskey and cough mixture. But already Mickey's bones are retreating from the surface of his skin. She turns to watch him, sitting on a dustsheet in the middle of the room, pushing the little red car she gave him back and forth across its creases. Evelyn hasn't asked where the money is coming from. Rosa is sure she hadn't even noticed that there was none, for a long time.

'Not now,' Rosa says. 'It's raining again. Come and have a look.'

Minutes later, Evelyn appears in the doorway. She is wearing a black silk nightie, stained at the collar, which swings around her cane-thin legs. Her nose is a puzzle of fine red lines. Her eyes are sunken, milky. She doesn't eat the food Rosa puts in front of her. Rosa waits until it goes cold or dry then eats it herself, standing over the kitchen counter.

'Well, well,' Evelyn says, clawing the doorframe to keep herself upright. 'Raining again. And on my last night, too. Did you know it was my last night tonight, Rosa darling?'

'I did.'

'Are you glad? Are you glad you'll get your dear mother back, all to yourself?'

'Yes,' Rosa answers. Her arms are folded over her chest. She squeezes them tight, to feel the points of tenderness in her breasts. In the bath, she had noticed the start of swelling.

'I don't think you are,' Evelyn says. 'I think you like having this lovely big apartment all to yourself. Do your friends come over when I'm at work? I bet they do. And I bet they say, "Well, look at this lovely big apartment. I wish my mother had played Shirley." Is that what they say, Rosa?'

'No one comes over,' Rosa says, turning back to the window, lips pressed white. Evelyn shudders across the room to join her. Finally, she catches herself on Rosa's shoulder. Rosa sees her yellowing, uncut nails from the corner of her eye.

'Then invite some people. I don't mind. I'll be out with Ray tonight, anyway, for the after-show party.'

'I might.'

'Good.' Evelyn plants a shaky kiss on the top of Rosa's head. When she tries to straighten up again, she loses her balance and Rosa has to wrap an arm around her waist to keep her steady. Through the thin silk, she is warm and clammy to the touch – like a new-born baby, Rosa imagines.

'Are you sure you can go on tonight? You don't have to.'

'Why wouldn't I?' Evelyn asks, and flinging her arm out to her side to grasp that imaginary ornament, she dips her head as though she is curtseying. She can't complete the movement. 'What will my fans think, darling, if I miss my last show?'

Rosa catches sight of the veins in her mother's raised arm – the clean blue of a summer sea. 'You're doing too much,' she says, looking away.

'It's the life,' Evelyn replies quietly.

Outside, it is just getting dark. People bustle up and down the street, black umbrellas bobbing above them. Mickey's toy car rattles as he pushes it. Now and then, he makes a gentle 'brumming' sound at the back of his throat.

'I hate it when it rains,' Evelyn says. 'It looks so sad.'

'No,' Rosa shakes her head. 'No, it doesn't look sad at all. You have to see past it, Ma. Look.' She points out how the city seems so much softer in the rain. The windows, the roofs, the wrought iron railings of the buildings opposite – they gleam like the jewellery Evelyn once owned when they're wet. Those umbrellas shift and shine like flocks of exotic birds. Rosa traces a fingertip down the patterns the raindrops create on the windows; they are ribbons, she thinks, as they run down and into each other. 'There are so many less people,' she says, 'when it rains.'

Evelyn pulls her closer. 'You don't get lonely?'

'No. I like it when it's just us – just me and you and Mickey,' Rosa answers. Then, taking Evelyn's hand, she wipes it over the misted glass. Deep down, she knows her mother is right. Close-up, the raindrops do start to look sad – like tears. And sometimes, just sometimes, Rosa can't bear to see them.

Clown's Shoes

Onstage again, you stare down at your feet, imagining you see the bright, painted curves of a pair of clown's shoes. This is how your audience views you: as nothing more than a performance; something to be seen and laughed at and then forgotten. It helps to pretend you are a clown, hidden inside baggy trousers, your true face invisible behind splashes of red lipstick and pale powder.

They sit before you in pairs, your audience, rows and rows of them, evening gowns and white bow ties glowing in the glare from the stage lights. It helps to pretend they cannot see so much of you. Though, by the midnight performance, when the society stoles and jewels have been replaced by students with hopeful hands and grubby mouths, you will not succeed in maintaining the illusion.

There is no pretending at that particular hour.

You do not want to be seen at all. This body was promised to someone else. This body, though, is all you have left to sell, and so you wear nothing now but a shadow, which you clutch over your chest as if this is the first time. While Thelma sings, you breathe your way, second by slow second, towards the moment when your disguise will be shone away. You think, when you can, of home.

Behind the locked door of your one rented room, amongst the strewn just-washed stockings and the long unstraightened bedsheets, your daughter sleeps, turning tangles into her coal-coloured hair. In the weak, early light, she will wake and you will sit her on your lap before the mirror and brush her curls smooth while she wriggles and winces. Then, once you are both dressed, you will usher her outside and return to the theatre, where Mama Swann will bring you and the other girls breakfast.

Your heart beats for your mornings with Lydia, watching her sitting on the stage-edge, swinging her legs over the pit and humming little tunes as she eats. Each night, though, you must make the same choice – between a door left open to possibilities, and a door which shuts her off from escape.

Your nightmares are filled with growing flames and shady intruders. So far, though, you have kept her safe. So far, that turned key has been worth the gamble.

She knows now that you leave her. She asks you why, and you tell her that you have a job, cleaning secretly for a lady who is too posh to do it herself. Sometimes, before you leave, she asks you to 'be' the posh lady, and you flounce around the room and pluck your drying clothes between your fingers and scrunch up your nose in exaggerated disgust. Then, Lydia laughs into her pillow until she cries, and her eyes close, and she says, 'Goodnight, Mammy.' She grows tired quickly. She is just four years old.

'Goodnight, Liddy-Bop,' you reply. Then you ease the door shut, creep downstairs, and walk a mile and a half through London's lamp-spotted depths to the theatre. You are excused, for the most part, from the day-time performances: Mama Swann pities your situation, and the other girls forgave you it, eventually, once Lydia had charmed them with her easy joy.

Tonight, the walk was bitter. Your breath made smoky plumes in front of you. Tonight, your skin was hard and blotched with cold as you undressed. Your undergarments, skirt, blouse and coat are hanging backstage now, arranged in the order they would sit on your body, as though you are still within them. Your shoes wait on the floor below. You need to feel you can slide directly back into them. You need to feel you never took them off.

Thelma finishes her song and immediately a spotlight strips

you. The audience gasps and giggles and whoops, then applauds. You count slowly to ten, hardly respiring, hating the unwanted thrill of standing naked before a packed, gargoyle crowd. This is the only intimacy you've known, since Danny.

The horror that precedes the performance is faded by the act, the same shift in feeling every night, but you do not wish to believe – as some of the girls do – that this is art. Your body was supposed to be a shrine, to the year you spent with Danny.

It still would be, if you could earn enough money to preserve it.

It was an audition board that brought you here, the black letters printed so boldly onto the white that you stopped and bundled Lydia inside and allowed her to be minded by Mama Swann – a stranger then, with a face folded into benevolence – while you stepped onto an empty stage. Watched from behind a cigar by a silent, middle-aged man, you unfastened your skirt and let it drop. When you unbuttoned your blouse and finally slipped your brassiere off, he stopped smoking and narrowed his eyes, considering whether your particular delineations were right for his show. He did not seem excited. He asked you to walk back and forth and turn around and repeat, and you did.

You were sure then you couldn't do it again.

He offered you solace, though, as you dragged your clothes back on, hands scrabbling. The law insisted you remain still for the duration of the nudity, he said; and that was why you agreed. Because already that day you had done worse. And because – though you were trying hard to ignore it, though you had tried to fill it with food and caring for your daughter and all manner of other things – you had recognised the deep hole Danny's lies had scooped out from your middle. Before you ever ducked inside the theatre in the unwelcome gloaming of a grey, hungry day, you knew that sensation. You were lonely. And it made you feel you had nothing to lose.

Even now, it is what persuades you to come back night after night.

The allotted time passes and you are thrust into shadow once more. Thelma will sing two more songs and then you will be displayed again, concealed initially behind a white-feathered fan, and then revealed, with the end-note, like some pearly fairground prize.

These days, there is a smallest part of you which anticipates this moment.

Two months ago, in the front row of the circle, suited and smiling, you saw him for the first time in nearly five years: brown-eyed and tall and as easy as his daughter. You saw him, eventually, recognise you. You saw that he was sitting with his wife. Wrapped in a fur, her diamond rings glistening in the darkling interior, her face was small and good and not at all what you wanted it to be.

You wondered then whether he, Danny, would see the change in your body and understand that you had grown his child.

And afterwards, you hunkered in the spindly stairwell shadows for too long and, when Mama Swann asked why you hadn't rushed home, refused to provide her with an answer. The truth was you were afraid: afraid of what the sight of him leaving would do to you. What if he offered his hand to his wife as she bent into their motorcar, as he had once offered it to you, when you danced across the floorboards of the attic room you were renting? What if, glancing through the window at you as he was driven away, he failed to spill over with regret? Because you had spilled over. You had flowed with the loss of him.

Now, he returns for the final number each night – alone. He sneaks into the aisle to your right, no doubt allowed late access by some monetary bribe, and stands in the dim slant of light the sign above the door casts, his top hat still in place, his gloved hands spired before him in the shape of prayer.

You do not need to see his face to know it's him. Your lips have measured his every dimension. They see the jutting shoulders and the breadth of smooth chest and the bony knees beneath his suit.

Some nights, you pull on your coat and shoes and run out into the street to catch him, still mostly naked. However many of the audience remain, though, he is never amongst them. You stand in the cold and watch people slip away; watch the lights in the café next door extinguished as the last of the theatre-goers disappear into the night; watch discarded tickets somersault over the pavements in the winter breeze. And still you expect that if you wait long enough, he will step out of the invisibility afforded him by an unlit doorway or a parked motorcar. But you cannot wait forever. Lydia is alone.

Other nights, you do not seek him at all. You are afraid of what speaking with him will mean. And tonight, as Thelma warbles through the second-to-last song, arms wide, chest generously bestowed, you decide, definitely and bravely, that you will never seek him out again. You have been made hard, by Lydia crying and begging you not to leave earlier this evening. And there is nothing to be gained in any case. He told you, when he had to, that he was to marry. You did not know then how real a claim you had to him. But your claim was undone, by a ceremony conducted distantly and in ignorance, and you must be resolute: as resolute as you were when you first came to London; or when you answered that audition board; or when you chose, though you were penniless and alone, to raise your daughter when some rich, doting couple might have taken her for their own with the right persuasion.

And yet, in spite of all this, you will keep his memory. You will return home, through the night's most dangerous hours, and lay down to sleep and imagine him present and happy in a room where only a little girl and a lost woman breathe, huddled together through dreams and nightmares.

You have always had a talent for imagining.

Thelma begins the last song and you position yourself for the scene, between the lamps which become, when viewed from a far enough distance, the bulbs around a dressing-room mirror. There is an enormous mirror angled behind you, and you have been taught to stand so that you can be seen only partially – the curve of a hip, the cup of a breast. You assume your pose and someone moves forward to hold the fan in place. You do not know which of the girls it is. Your eyes are already fixed on that spot, by the door, where Danny will appear. You begin again your routine of fancying the most ridiculous clothes onto your bare skin: the wide hoop of a pair of striped trousers; the twang of braces about your shoulders; the too-big slap of the shoes bulging out in front of you.

And when finally he appears, you do something you are bound against: you push the fan aside, you step forward out of the gloom, and you let him see you. All of you. Because this, his gaze, is all you have left of him. You cannot relinquish that last treasure. And though you have bound yourself now against hoping for him, you have to ask of him this one promise – that so long as you stand here, naked onstage, he will come back to stand opposite you.

Your heart clatters around in your chest as you wait for his answer. For a moment, you think he will turn and walk out, embarrassed by you. But, just as the girls move forward to curl the fan around you again, he takes his hat from his head and, face straight and honest, bows to you, just as he did the very first time you met.

At your middle, you feel the promise – a tight, brilliant flare – and you smile into the dark. Then, because you must, you resume your pose and, glancing down at your bare feet, imagine you see the bright, painted curves of a pair of clown's shoes.

Moon Dog

Bob hears the bell rattle from the storeroom and, pressing a thick hand against the box of books he's unpacking, uncurls into a standing position – a question mark becoming an exclamation mark. He checks the face of the grandfather clock his wife makes him hide in the back. It's the right time. Wiping his dusty hands in the seat of his trousers, he steps through to the shop, then, smiling at the man – because, yes, he is a man now – by the door, he takes a seat behind the counter and, with a sigh, lets his shoulders crumple down towards his stomach until he is curled up and contented as a cat.

Bob's shop always has brought him a certain kind of peace. Dorothy has never understood it, and Bob doesn't want to explain it to her, but the soft curves of the violins and guitars he mounts on the walls make him think of the sea; of the waves that rode past his childhood home. The pianos' shiny surfaces, too, please him. He polishes them until his customers can see themselves at the keys: until he, when he plays them to the empty shop before opening, can see himself there; a boy again, reflected in the glassy surface of a rock pool.

'Hello there,' Bob says.

The man at the door doesn't look at Bob. He keeps his hood pulled up like a monk, and with swift, repeated movements of his heavy hands, straightens the shelved books so that they overlap each other by a perfect inch. Bob knows those movements intimately.

'You don't have to do that,' he says.

'I know.'

'Then why not just leave it for today?'

'Can't.'

Bob picks up the cup of tea he made two hours ago and swills it about; watches it whirl around an invisible central island. He places the cup back on the counter and inspects his watch: the second hand is stuttering past the six. He'll give it until the o'clock before he speaks again.

But today, it is Angus who goes first.

'Did you know,' he says, his eyes and hands on the second shelf now, 'that beaked whales don't like sonar?'

'Really?' Bob replies. Sensing that this could be a long one, he lifts his newspaper from underneath the counter, snaps it open, and spreads it across his lap. Angus nods his head: it's like watching a guillotine drop.

'Studies have shown that naval sonar exercises lead to haemorrhaging and stranding. I've written some letters.'

'Who to?'

'The Queen, the Prime Minister, the First Sea Lord.'

'The first –'

'… Sea Lord. Head of the Royal Navy.'

Bob hums. He uses the sound, as he did when his son was a boy, to create a space in which to think. He knows better than to push Angus on this. 'And if they don't write back?' he asks, finally.

'I'll start a protest,' Angus says.

It's the answer Bob didn't want. 'Is that a good idea, after last time?'

'They wouldn't have arrested me if it wasn't true.'

He finishes rearranging the books and sidesteps nearer to the counter; stops at the resins. He still has the hood of his coat pulled over his head, though the sun is strong today and Bob can't guess at why he put it on in the first place. Beneath its cave-like rim, Bob can see only the triangular tip of his nose and the dash of his pressed mouth. He notices that Angus hasn't shaved in a few days. Hairs sprout from his chin like weeds.

'Shall I get you a cup of tea? Angus?'

Angus shakes his head, too fast, like a dog drying itself. He has three rows of resins lined up already, the corners of each two by three inch box touching the very tips of the next. There must be a hundred boxes in that basket. Bob wanders across to the phone and lifts it from the cradle. Dorothy will be making herself lunch now. He could ring her, ask her to come over and talk to Angus. Dorothy might be able to make him forget about the whales.

'I saw something excellent on the way over.'

Bob hooks the receiver back onto the cradle and waits for Angus to continue.

'It's been there since this morning. Do you want to see it?'

'What is it?'

'Excellent,' Angus repeats.

Bob rethinks the question. '*Where* is it?'

Angus raises one hand and points at the door, his head still bent over the basket of resins. 'Outside,' he says.

Bob focuses on his pointed finger. Two long windows front the shop, and he can feel the sun pushing through them, spraying strings of light along the edges of his violins. It makes them appear circular, like the two stacked blobs of a snowman's body. He pictures the shop from the outside, as though he is a customer. The lettering informing people that this is *Bob's Music Box* must look like gold today. The instruments, too, will be shining like jewels. Yes, he'd like to go outside.

'It might not still be there,' Bob says.

'Well, let's find out.'

Bob lifts the paper from his lap and lays it, face down like a dead bird, over the counter, then grabs his coat from the back of his chair. As he steps towards the door, he glances, just once, back at the telephone.

He always promises to ring Dorothy if Angus comes in.

One day, he thinks, he might.

***

Standing on the pavement outside the shop, Bob pushes his hands into his pockets and takes a good deep in-breath. Though it is long minutes away, he can smell the sea from here. Sometimes, he fancies he can hear it, too, but he knows he can't really. This is the closest he's ever managed to get Dorothy to the sea; the closest he ever will get her. She can't abide the coast. The screams of the seagulls – 'sea rats' she calls them – give her the horrors.

'We need to go further down the road,' Angus explains after a moment's deliberation. 'It'll be best from there.'

Bob listens to their footsteps as they walk. Their rhythm, he's pleased to notice, still matches; their steps have grown heavier these last few years. He crosses his eyes to watch the steam that twists out of his nostrils diffuse. Over breakfast this morning, he'd predicted that snow was coming. Dorothy had disagreed. 'Frost that comes to nothing,' was what they were in for, she'd said, and patted his shoulder as she'd scurried past – the same way she used to pat Angus's shoulder when he sat to a meal.

'Did you know,' Angus says, 'that there were a group of medieval people who lived in Scotland called the Picts?'

'Is that right?'

'Yes. And historians can't decide whether they were tattooed all over or not. They can't decide. Did you know that?'

'No, I didn't.'

Angus nods that singular, abrupt nod of his. 'I read it.'

'What else have you read?' Bob asks.

'About a thousand things,' Angus answers.

As they walk further away from the shop, Bob starts to fidget. He didn't lock the door. Not that he's ever heard of Picton Road having any problems with crime, but you never know. You never do know. He learned that lesson too late in life.

'How far are we going, Gus?'

'Not far.'

Picton Road is broad, and, Bob considers, just a tad Americanised these days. He hates the word, but each shop is painted a different jaunty pastel colour – American sorts of colours, he thinks – and tiny silver tables keep appearing outside cafés, and there's even a dinky coffee cart parked on the pavement now; a man with a pyramid shaped hat inside. Americanised is the only word for it. In the summer, Bob can almost imagine he's strolling down a Connecticut shopping street as he walks the last stretch of the two miles from his front door to the shop.

But on days like this, when the winter sun is shining the streets cold, and there are few people to tolerate, his little America doesn't seem so bad. Though he wants to disapprove of the changes – he thinks he should disapprove of them, at his age – he can't. On days like this, he experiences flashes, instants, when he thinks he's standing on the very spot in the whole world that he ought to be.

Really, this is just the kind of place he'd imagined growing grey in when he was first married and still young enough to be romantic. Here a man could build a family business, pass it on to his son. Here a man had the freedom to begin a whole new tradition.

It still saddens him that he'd had to give up on that idea.

At Angus's direction, they turn left at the end of the road and, a couple of paces later, slow to a stop. Bob's chest is heaving from walking at Angus's pace. For a second, he crouches down and presses his hands to his knees, compacting like a fold-away table. Feeling Angus's eyes on him, he rolls back up again sooner than he'd like. They're facing out of town towards the neighbouring farmland. The town's shops, houses, people, are all at their backs.

'This is it.' Angus flings his arm diagonally away from his body then lets it drop back to his side, as though he's a puppet with an indecisive master.

Bob traces the sweep of his arm. 'I don't know what I'm looking at,' he says.

'They're called parhelia.'

'What are?'

'The three suns,' Angus huffs. He grabs his father's hand and thrusts it forwards, as if teaching a child a simple fact. Bob notices that his hand is a withered claw between Angus's fleshy fingers, and looks away. 'See. See how, if you look at the sun, there's another sun on either side of it. See that..? It's a natural phenomenon.'

Bob nods. The boy is right. The sun seems to be sitting with two smaller friends, who imitate its trembling form. Linking them is a long, thin chain of circular light. Bob tries to look directly at them, but can't. So bright are the three suns that they make the rest of the sky look dark, as though dusk is gate-crashing midday. Bob crosses his arms over his chest. He is glad the town is so quiet as he stands with his son and looks into the sky. A passing car or a walker would have ruined this... This what? It's something primordial, he thinks; a glimpse of something ancient and universal. But it's private, too. It's the very first time, it seems, that he and Angus have communicated.

Years ago, Bob had tried to assemble this kind of exchange, with toys and lessons and conversation. He'd sat little Angus next to him on his piano stool and demanded that he tap out nursery rhymes with one stiff, angry digit. But Angus has chosen his own way, and this is it. Bob reaches over, pinches the back of his hood between thumb and finger, and pulls it slowly off. In the sunlight, clusters of silver strands spring out from Angus's black hair.

'They're called parhelia,' he explains again. 'Or sun dogs.'

'Why sun dogs?'

'I don't know.'

'Good name, though.'

Bob glances at Angus, at the wide cheeks which dwarf his totem pole features, and notices that his eyes are watering. He's staring too intently at the suns. And that, Bob thinks, has always been Angus's problem – he sees only one thing at a time. Though the town looks like a postcard today, Angus has no interest in the slate roofs which glint against the shivering sky, or the fields that climb away from the coast in a bid to escape the lingering, diamond-frost. He has no concern for people or beauty or time. Bob though, can't help but glance at his watch. He didn't lock the shop.

'Don't do that,' he says. 'It'll make you go blind.'

Angus appears not to have heard. Bob knows he would never respond to such a nonsensical statement. It has always been Bob's habit, though – a habit he learned from his own father – to break these moments. He cringes when Dorothy reminds him of all the times he dragged Angus away from one thing or another because they were *in a rush* or they *had to get home*. They probably hadn't needed to; not really.

He remembers, most clearly, standing on the beach with Angus and Dorothy when Angus was about eight, and being in the most furious temper. It was raining, and the sky and the sea and the sand were all the same ill-grey colour, but Angus had wanted to see the crabs, and so they had gone. Once there, Angus had refused to go home until he had watched one particular orange dot scuttle all the way back into the waves. As far as Bob knew, that might never happen, and so after an hour of waiting, he had picked the child up and hauled him back to the car. Angus had screamed all the way, hammering his hands and feet into his father's marshmallow body.

It had been Dorothy's turn then, to be furious. 'Why can't you be patient, for once?' she'd asked through flat lips from the passenger seat. 'Why can't you just *understand* him?'

Bob feels he is learning to now. Forty years too late.

71

He looks again at his son. Angus stands perfectly still but for the tears that stumble down his face. His wide chest doesn't even seem to rise and fall under his bulky coat. Just now he is as intense and as sure as those suns. He too, looks inert. He too, is burning. He is a third sun dog.

'You know,' Bob says, more to himself than to Angus. 'You remind me of a sun dog.'

He feels himself blush. This is the kind of sentiment he never shared with his own father; the kind he'd never intended to share with Angus. Immediately, he wishes he hadn't said it.

'How?' Angus replies.

'What?'

'How?'

Bob hadn't been expecting to have to answer – he fumbles around his slowing brain for something to say. Twenty years ago he would have found his words easily. Ten years ago, even. Not now. One day not too far away, he thinks, Angus will wander into *Bob's Music Box* and a new owner will ask him to leave.

'Because you're rare,' Bob answers.

'Moon dogs are rarer than sun dogs,' Angus says. 'Perhaps I should remind you of a moon dog.'

'Perhaps you're right. Have you ever seen a moon dog?'

Angus shakes his head.

'Do you think you might?'

'It's not impossible.'

'I'd like to see one.'

'If I see one, I'll show you,' Angus promises.

'Thank you,' Bob answers, allowing himself the first smile of the day, because that is enough. A promise is more than Angus has ever given Dorothy, and she always knew him so much better. It's a promise Bob doesn't deserve. 'Now, I've got to get back to the shop, okay? Angus? Is that okay?'

Angus nods his head. 'I'm staying here,' he says.

***

As he reaches the shop door, Bob turns to see if there is any sign of Angus following him. The street is as empty as old age: there is just the little cart, winking in the sun and puffing its steam. He pushes through the door and, stepping behind the counter, unhooks the phone from the wall. His fingers dial Dorothy independently. She sounds old when she answers.

'He's been in,' Bob tells her.

'Been and gone?'

'Yep.'

'Why didn't you ring me?'

'I am.'

'Earlier.'

'He was only here a second. There wasn't time.'

'Okay then,' she sighs. Bob imagines he can hear her lifting a sandwich off her plate then returning it without taking a bite, the inaudible sound of untouched tea going cold. He imagines her rubbing her hand over her papery forehead and closing her eyes, angry that yet again her son has chosen her husband over her. Bob feels the pluck of guilt deep at his core, like a violin string snapping.

'Will you go over tonight?' he asks. He says it to drown the silence. He regrets it immediately. He knows too well the way her face twists when she thinks about visiting her son; the way her fading lips shift across her cheek.

'No. Probably not,' she mutters. 'You know he hates us disturbing him there.'

'Mmm.'

'Maybe he'll come in tomorrow.'

'Maybe. He might stay longer tomorrow.'

'Yes, he might,' Dorothy says. 'What time will you be ready for dinner?'

Bob glances at the grandfather clock. Months ago, and following many trials, he'd managed to find a way to angle it so that it was visible from both the shop and the storeroom. That way, he's sure never to miss Angus. Tomorrow, he knows, when the hands touch quarter to one, Angus will come in and straighten the books by the front door. Bob reminds himself, for the third time that day, to take the time after closing to push some of those books onto their sides, to thrust his hand into the basket of resins and toss them around. Only then, at a couple of minutes past five, can he start the walk home.

'Around quarter to six,' he tells his wife.

He spends the next hour watching the street. Angus has to pass the shop again to return to his flat and Bob is hoping that he'll call back in, to tell him something else about the sun dogs, or suggest they go hunting for moon dogs tonight. It's never happened before, though. Angus has only ever come in at exactly quarter to one.

Eventually, Bob catches sight of him. He's marching along on the opposite side of the road, his right hand flapping at his side as usual – like a wing. Angus always looks like he's trying to fly away. He doesn't pause as he passes the shop. Bob raises his arm to wave, but Angus doesn't see; he has pulled his hood back over his head.

'Gus,' Bob calls. 'Gus!'

Angus doesn't hear. He rushes along, head down, and is gone before Bob has even lowered his waving arm.

Sitting again, Bob drags the newspaper onto his lap, but he doesn't read a word of it. He sips at his cold tea. It's like living by the sea, he thinks. Yes, that's it. It's like living by the sea: the tide comes in, the tide goes out, and you've got absolutely no control in the matter. No control at all. You just have to wake each morning and wait to see if the waves will come your way.

Paper Birds

Only after her husband has started the motorcar and chugged away down the long crooked drive does Analese move to the window. She knows the timing of it now, from the first grumble of its engine to the moment its shuddering grey roof finally disappears from view. She counts three minutes on the gold mantelpiece clock, then stands and drifts towards the glass to wait. There is comfort in this – the smooth familiarity of waiting. She has been waiting for one thing or another her entire life.

This morning, she looks out on a burly autumn sky. The sun shapes a high, hard circle, and all around the house sharp shadows cast through the dust-flecked rooms. Some days, when the clouds sag low and glum, Analese feels she could open the long sash windows and push her hand straight into them; that she could climb on top of one and float away. But she only watches, and waits for him to come – the man who stands at the gate.

She straightens up, puts her hands to her waist and tries to make the slim points of her fingers touch as she searches for her image in reflection. Unable to find it, she turns to the oval mirror across the room, but great chutes of sunlight decorate its gilt edges and the candlesticks and the vases and all the other little trinkets peppered about before it, and the surface does nothing but push the sun's heat back out through the window.

Analese is invisible.

Sighing, she considers the street. The grounds of the house are edged by a fence, as tall as the rows of trees which guard the pavements beyond, and Analese looks out through its metal posts. She barely sees them now. She does not feel them, closing in on her, as she did that first wet day when her new husband drove her through the front gate. It was the first time she'd been in a motorcar, and she had spent so long peering out at the wobbly grey aspect of what she was passing that she had not seen what was in front of her. He had brought her to some sort of government building, she thought as he stopped the engine; perhaps he was calling at work. But when he turned to smile at her, his big hand pressed to the back of her seat, she understood that this was to be her new home.

She scans the street quickly, resting her eyes in each place for only a fraction of a second, like a bee tasting a flower before bumbling away to try another.

Analese feels she always moves this way now, since he started coming to the house. At first she was sure her husband would notice her fidgeting and suspect something. But Charles has said nothing. He never looks at her properly any more, and Analese is glad of it.

A small brown bird skitters down onto the lawn, pecks at the grass once, twice, as though it is bowing to an audience, then hops through a gap in the fence and flutters away. Analese watches it sail up through the stippled tree canopy. She watches until it becomes a black spot on the empty sky, and she wonders if birds ever feel lonely. She doesn't imagine so. Birds are built for freedom, after all; and freedom, she supposes, has always been a lonely sort of business.

She sighs again, louder this time, just to hear a sound in the room apart from that endlessly even ticking and tocking.

Through the gate, she has a view of three or four of the houses which stand beyond in a wide, delicate curve. In the morning light they are bright and pleasant, and Analese thinks she might like to live in one of them. Then, on days like today, she could fling open the windows without anyone complaining about draughts or finger-smudges; she could gather flowers from the garden and thrust them into old jars and line them up all along the sills; she could skip down the front steps and stride along the street in a loose cotton dress and feel the cold air rush up her nose and all about her brain.

She rests her elbows on the sill – this wide, empty, real one.

She knows he will stop outside the house with the door painted racing green. He will be wearing a charcoal suit and hat, and a red tie which sits on his chest like a bared heart. He will be holding a newspaper, he always is, but he won't read it. He will only stare up at her window, and today his eyes will be narrowed against the brilliance.

She knew him right away, of course, that first day he came to the gate. They had shared a cup of tea together – nothing more, to begin with – when she and her husband had taken that trip to Bath last year. Charles had disappeared after breakfast each day, to 'talk business' he said, and Analese was left to wander the hotel; to amble around the elliptical lake, or sip tea in the ornamental gardens. Without invitation, he sat opposite her at her table and poured more tea from the pot, and as the day warmed he stayed and nodded along as she lied in response to every question he asked her.

She was embarrassed, she remembers, by the elaborate protrusion of her skirt. It was one of Charles's favourites.

From her window, she cannot see the fans of wrinkles which spread from the corner of each of his eyes, but she remembers them. She remembers too the way the shifting light turned the dark hairs on his arms to garnet. As he moved the tea things around and absently folded a pair of wings into a white napkin, Analese had watched his hands, and for a brief moment she had allowed his to meet hers on the embroidered tablecloth.

That was where it began, with that most tentative movement,

and even now she remembers thinking that his touch felt too light, far too light. Charles's hands weighed so much more.

The first time he arrived at the house, she feared he would come to the door and try to speak with her. But, no; he had done exactly nothing. He has done nothing every day since, except stand and watch her at the window. He watches her like she is an animal at the zoo. And when he walks away, he leaves her like an animal; a tiger perhaps, declawed or lame, that can only stare at the space outside its cage and wonder at why men can move so freely and other animals cannot.

What she does not understand, though, is what he wants from her. She has given him everything he could possibly have desired, pressed against a tree in a secret, shaded spot, her breath held in fear of discovery. And she is, after all, already twenty-three years old: threads have started to appear in the skin around her eyes and mouth, as though her stitching is coming loose.

She folds the edge of the curtain over itself and drags her fingers down the length of the doubled fabric, fast, so that it burns her skin. She invents these little ways to injure herself occasionally, just mildly: a shard of shattered wineglass pricking a fingertip; a picture frame knocked over to land on a bared foot. These things are just enough to make her collect herself when she thinks of it – the hard push of the tree at her back; the layers of her skirt, gathered up all around her like the petals of some gigantic blossom.

Nevertheless, she thinks of what they did more and more. She wills it to happen again. Likely, she considers, some sort of disease has infiltrated her mind, because the next ridiculous idea seems to chase after the last. One day, when the rain fell thick and sleek and still he appeared, his suit turning black in patches, the rim of his hat producing waterfalls, she almost opened the window and hung out to call to him. Even worse, she spent one busy dawn planning to walk to the gate and speak to him through the slats. But she had known, deep down, that if she ventured that far she would unlock the gate and invite him inside. And she was worried about what to say. However innocent-sounding her words, the staff were sure to report them to her husband, and she would become a scandal then, for the sake of sharing with a gentleman in a charcoal suit what she suspected every husband in Europe shared with maids and widows and friends and strangers alike.

But, maybe, she can't help thinking. Maybe one day. And her mind strays again to the idea she has had and dismissed a thousand times already: she will write him a letter, and it will include a time and a place, and when he comes, she will throw the letter from the window and it will swoop down to him. It is a silly idea, she knows that. How would she ever get it to fly in the right direction? But she can't shake it from her mind, the image of that flat white envelope gliding towards him; of him catching it and tearing it open and reading it with darting eyes; of him removing his hat and, making sure no one is watching, blowing a promise to her in a kiss.

Sometimes, on those nights when Analese dreams, she dreams of hundreds of tiny, winged envelopes plunging off her window ledge and into the air. She dreams of them whirling around outside the house, looping back and forth through the fence as easily as air itself. She dreams they have his name written on their backs.

She allows herself to glance at the mantle clock once more. Eight minutes yet until he comes. Nine hours or more before Charles returns. A touch over twelve hours before she takes to her bed and lies and prays that Charles will not join her before she sleeps. She moves to her desk and pulls out a fresh sheet of paper and a heavy, silver-nibbed pen, then she goes back to the window and sets them upon the sill.

She could do it. She could press wings into the paper, as he did his napkin that day. She could throw it, just as carelessly as he had, and watch it glide away. She lifts two corners between her thumbs and forefingers. Outside, a single leaf is released from a branch and spirals towards the ground. Analese pauses to watch it, and its fall is so graceful, so easy, that momentarily the sight halts the billowing hope within her. Her own fall will not be so gentle. She flattens the paper back onto the sill and returns her hands to her waist. But she knew, that day, what it was to want hands upon her! She knew it! And yes – she shakes her head at the simplicity of it – she knows it still! She cannot give up on it. With a grunt of determination, she snatches up the pen once more and begins, without a thought for the words, to write. When he arrives, she will be ready. Yes, when he arrives she will be waiting, and she will launch her paper birds into flight, and she hopes, she hopes – no, she believes – that soon he will teach her what it means to fly with them.

The Saddest Jazz

A muzzy indoors electric glow, the blue colour of trouble, illuminates parts of the bar. Against the far wall, one of those old-fashioned microphones waits – silver, black-slatted, big enough to hide half a face behind. Standing at it, smaller than ever, deep red hair curling down to her shoulders and each coil shining a different hue in the downlights, is Hattie James. Her face is paler than the whites of her eyes. Her skin feels thin as paper. Her breath comes in shallow, shallow puffs.

She's less than she ought to be. She's forgotten everything.

Tom, her husband, sits close in the front row; close enough to touch. But in the shadows she feels he is miles away, years away, a lifetime away. Hattie searches for her starting note – an A flat, slouching below middle C. Amongst the chatter and the chinking glasses, it's lost to her. She tries sounding it low in the back of her throat, her vocal chords quivering. She tries ascending and descending a scale. No. Only major intervals reveal themselves. The sorrowful bends of the minors, silenced by her nerves, are gone.

Hattie looks for the crest of Tom's head, the denser brush of beard over his chin. There's reassurance there. She finds his twitching smile at the edge of her spotlight's wide disc.

She promised herself she'd tell him tonight, after her performance. Now, though, the timing's wrong.

It was Tom's idea to come. She'd be doing them a favour, he'd said, and Hattie suspected he'd set the whole sorry thing up – Charlie's Bar, centre of town, packed Tuesday through to Sunday, wouldn't struggle to find a singer – but she hadn't questioned it. Tom was right. She didn't want to give it up. It was the fear that had stopped her, that first time the notes fell away and every song, every word, slipped, became a fraction less clear.

Hattie scans the room. It's still filling up. People climb the steps from the puddled street and shuffle through the door in the opposite wall, shaking their heads, swiping at each other's shoulders, unpeeling their coats. Raindrops spark up on them like thousands of fairy lights.

Outside, Hattie knows, the rain is flowing over the guttering of every roof and cascading down walls to hammer the pavements; the wind is squealing against the low, heavy sky. When she and Tom had arrived, they'd jumped from the car and made a run for it, the coats they held over their heads flapping like flimsy flags. They'd dodged an empty dustbin, upturned and rolling aimlessly about, and finally flung themselves inside.

It was a night for jazz, Hattie thought then. The saddest jazz.

At the bar, a woman in a black lace dress sits swaying. As cables are dragged past, Hattie watches her swing, perilous, on her bar stool, steadied only by the familiar sloshing of a drink. She's sixty, maybe. Glum. But attractive, too; definitely that. She drinks and drinks and waits and waits for someone to notice her. And as Hattie watches, the lost note returns – an A flat, sagging near the bottom of her range.

A switch is flicked and the microphone buzzes into life.

'Hello,' Hattie begins. 'I'm Hattie James.' Most of the room turns towards her as Patrick, her pianist, dashes out an introductory smattering of trills and mordents. Hattie nods him into the opening chords.

The notes wind off her tongue then. Hattie doesn't think about them; she doesn't need to. In the front row, Tom leans forward and, thumbs up, pumps his fists at her. At this, Hattie grins stupidly. Three years and then some and still his presence in a room is as physical for her as the surge of the sea, that frenzied crash to the coast.

Last night, the sea had flooded her dreams. In the comfort of the sleeping dark, she'd told him already and he was angry not at her but for her, and they were driving, shaping hectic turns on swerving roads, to the coast, where he made her watch as wave after wave slumped onto the sand. 'Look at that,' he said. 'Just look.' And Hattie tried only to look – a point of tension, pulsing in Tom's neck, was coaxing her to obey – but it was no use. 'It's no good,' she said. 'I can still hear it. It'll be different when I can't hear it!' Tom, circling her, pressed two steady hands over her ears then. But still there was something. A deep, dark reverberation: her heart beating, perhaps.

She woke, abruptly, into thick, tacky darkness. Pressing her head to Tom's heart, she listened for its unplayable rhythm. When he wriggled towards her, though, and arranged her in the familiar curve of his arm, she couldn't help but snap.

Tom held up his hands in surrender, head lifting off the pillow. 'What? What did I do?'

'Nothing. I just need to listen.'

'How do I sound, Doctor James?' he replied. And that's when she should have told him, while he was half asleep, mentioning a doctor, but she hadn't been able.

'Reliable,' she'd said.

And truly that's all she hopes for now – that he'll carry on being reliable. At eighteen, she'd thought a marriage should be exciting. At twenty-eight, there is Tom, and Hattie doesn't want anything more than what she knows: Tom, grumbling when the news comes on but insisting on watching it anyway; Tom, talking endlessly about starting his own business but never finding the courage to do it; Tom, refusing always to throw out holey socks. These are the things she believes in.

Last week, when Tom was working late, she'd knelt at their

bedside and prayed he wouldn't change when she did. It was the first time she'd prayed since the frail, empty hopes – those most hopeful hopes, really – of childhood.

Hattie takes her break and tags along with Patrick when he steps down the stairs and outside. Standing in the doorway, she cups her hands round his lighter flame, then watches the burning point of his cigarette dance in the dark. Moody purple clouds clamber and crawl across the sky. A crow squawks a string of black notes into the confusion, but their tune is undone by the slapping wind.

'So?' Patrick asks.

'It wasn't so bad.'

Tom pushes himself into the narrow doorway, touching his warm palm to her back, and Hattie smiles. Before they were married, she would walk pressed close to find the thrill of that beautifully predictable hand, then, laughing, step just out of reach, forcing him to move with her. She didn't want him to know it, but even then, she'd needed to feel him there.

'Really?' he asks.

'Really,' she answers.

Whenever Tom speaks, Hattie tries to recall the words, all the words they spoke in the early months. There won't be enough time now to exchange all they want to offer. And she wants to remember but she can't. Already, her memories run like silent movies. There'll be no chance of finding the sounds when she's been deaf for a year, or two, or ten. Hattie closes her eyes and, ignoring the yellow shapes writhing behind her lids, breathes slowly through her nose, calming the panic that rises and swirls in her. Deaf. Deafness. Such small, enormous words.

'So you'll come back next week?' Tom says. Hattie nods. Yes, she must. Somewhere, jammed between the notes and the lyrics there's her, herself, the tight-packed essence of Mrs Hattie James. She's sung since she was a six year old. She took two prickly, short-tempered months out and didn't know herself. But tonight, she's right again. Right, then, is what she'll lose.

'Good.' Tom pecks at her ear lobe. 'Drink?'

'Please.'

Jiggling around, staying warm, Patrick sucks on his cigarette and rolls his eyes.

'What?' Hattie laughs.

'You two,' he says, sending smoky serpents to the roofs. 'He didn't even ask what you wanted.'

'He knows.'

'Exactly.'

Hattie twists around to watch Tom rising away from her. The thin wedges of his shoulder blades point through his cotton T-shirt; his arms dangle loose at his sides as his right-hand fingers drum unknown beats against his thigh; the crown of his hair stabs outwards, always outwards, like the petals of a sunflower. Yes, she knows that man. And he her. There's nothing surer. But he disappears around the doorframe, and as he does, doubt assumes his place. It descends fast, like long-learnt knowledge, along a hurtling glissando. Tom could leave.

'It really is enough to make you –' Patrick takes one last cigarette puff, then flicks the butt into a puddle and watches it sizzle out. 'Ill.'

Hattie turns back, frowning. As quickly as it appeared, the idea dissolves and is lost, in that same easy way dreams are upon waking. She loses the sense, the certainty of it. But its remnants linger as Patrick shuffles her back inside. They tighten around her heart, like a gripping hand.

Doubt. Hattie reaches to touch the deep, lumpy sound with her tongue. Doubt. Even the word is an ugly sensation.

She sings like she's never sung before. Every note brings a taste, a texture, and Hattie savours them. There are no loose grace notes, no throwaway phrases. And as she sings, she searches for the shape of every syllable Tom ever pushed or curled or spat from his mouth; the thickness of his just-waking voice; the tuneless songs he hurls around the shower. There's no way of knowing if she'll remember them, these richest things, when words are reduced to silent black designs.

She hadn't been brave enough to ask the doctor for timescales. Instead, she's set her own limits. When Tom's voice fades to a faint thing, she's decided, she'll stop singing.

Now, Tom catches her eye and they grin. They've only known the good parts, so far.

The night he proposed, Hattie had lain awake, trekking her mind in search of the so many ways he might hurt her. But this, she couldn't have anticipated. And the worst of it is, there's nothing she can do to stop it. She'd rather not have known. Even the best intentions won't stop him growing distant. And he could – he could wash away entirely, quite accidentally, on a sea of sound.

She'll swim after him, though, she thinks. She will, even if it drowns her.

Patrick's fingers weave up and down the keys to signal her last song. A slow four-four, starting on a G. Hattie seeks the woman at the bar again. Eyes closed, she's shifting with the music – her head, her hands, her hips. There's something about her. Something fascinating and melancholy. Later, Hattie decides, she'll go and ask her for the private, buried things: if she's ever sung jazz; where her life went wrong. Because she can see now, how easy it would be to become her. How easy it must be, ending up alone.

Already she's found reasons for lying. She gets in the car and goes and somehow it's necessary, the most necessary far-down thing, to lie; to sit behind rained-on windows, fingers around sound, and turn it up and down, up and down. She has filled hours with fluctuating radio noise; secret hours that'll surely lead to more.

'Isn't there a cure?' That was the one real question she had asked the doctor. And he'd said there were options, options worth looking at, things that might help, but that nothing was guaranteed.

The song ends on a low G. Hattie breathes through it. She doesn't quite have control of it. As the applause starts, she notices Tom standing to peer across the room and follows his eyes. Behind the bar, a man is waving, nodding. They're up to something. Hattie doesn't have chance to imagine what it might be though, because nearby a sharp crack sounds. She snaps back her head. Above, there is a swinging movement, an opening, and then a million slivers of colour are falling, falling.

Hattie watches them come, the rose and azure, cream and magenta, jade and daffodil and violet – any and every shade, cut and tucked into tiny tendrils – and she names them, because this is her newest habit, to find the most specific names for things, to test the words. But there are too many to see all at once, and she holds out her palms and she gathers them, the paper bow-ties.

'Thomas James,' she whispers. 'You clever man.'

It's something they watched together, months ago. An old cabaret, airing late one night. It had ended like this, the last act standing in showering colour, and Hattie had said she wanted to end a show like that, just once, before it all stopped; before she stopped.

'You'll never stop,' Tom had mumbled.

And Hattie had answered the only way she could. 'Maybe I'll have to,' she'd said. 'Maybe, some time, I'll have to.'

As the flow of colours slows, Hattie bunches her hands into fists to catch the last pieces. Tom must know, she thinks; he must know something. She glances at Patrick – who winks – then back at Tom. Tom's face is serious. When they get home, she'll check the drawer she thought he wouldn't open; the drawer she stuffed the doctor's leaflets into. He must have discovered her written-down secrets.

'Tom,' she says again. And uncurling her hands and looking down, Hattie sees she's trapped just one of his paper tendrils: a twirl of bright blood red. A heartbeat, she thinks, and she's smiling, she realises, smiling free all those tears she's been swallowing for so long. It looks just like a heartbeat.

Running for Bernie

Bernard Percy Russell III – named for 'is father, and 'is father before 'im – 'ad enjoyed the smooth, tactile weight of 'is 'eredity the first time 'e was 'anded the brush. Aged three, chubby 'ands making fists around the long, wooden 'andle, naked feet shuffling over the pavement outside 'is own front door, 'e'd grinned at the 'ard rasp of it against the paving stones. It was a sound you could dance to. And 'e 'ad, clapped on by 'is parents, who'd smiled to see 'im learning so young what 'is future would feel like.

At fourteen, Bernie pretends 'e 'as no sense of that memory, though it's still there, somewhere deep down; an image. Except now 'e thinks that brush as stinking as the still-'ot body of a new-dead rat, as shaming as 'is mother wiping something off 'is cheek in the street, as 'eavy as the anchors of the ships 'e sees at the docks, when 'e 'appens there on business. It drags 'im down – just like it did 'is father, and 'is father before 'im.

That's why Bernie started running.

'Might get you into trouble this, boy,' Garrott 'ad warned 'im that first time they'd met. It was 'is interview, 'is test. Mr Garrott was smiling and agreeable and – Bernie soon learnt – acting. Garrott is mad as a starving dog when 'e chooses to be.

'D'you know 'ow to get yourself out of a sticky situation?' 'e'd asked.

'I do, Sir,' Bernie'd answered. And Garrott 'ad switched then, quick as a blink, and slapped Bernie's 'ead, 'ard, so that 'is earlobe stung and swelled into a rose petal.

'Tell me *how*,' 'e ordered.

'By running, Sir,' Bernie'd said. 'By running.' It was the first thing came to 'is mind. It was what 'e 'imself wanted to do now 'e'd been properly introduced to Mr Garrott. It got 'im the job, though. Garrott 'ad laughed out this short, 'orsey sort of a snort, then wrapped 'is arm around Bernie's shoulders.

'Tomorrow,' 'e said, patting Bernie roughly on the back before swaying away. 'Soon as it gets dark... And don't be late, boy.'

'E didn't ask for a name.

That was nearly two years ago and Bernie still 'asn't told Garrott 'is real name. There's no need. 'E's someone different every night: Davy or Lad or Betsy. And anyway, the only time Garrott sees 'is boys is when 'e's three sheets to the proverbial, and they've learnt to stay a few feet distant then; out of arm's reach. They push 'is takings to 'im across the same sticky table at the back of the Hat and Feathers. There, they're just another thin face in the gloom, 'cause it's a dingy old place, the Hat and Feathers, stuck in between the ironmongers and that drapers' shop what was boarded up years past. Bernie 'as seen live rats there, string-tailed and bony-backed, scuttling about in the shadows of illicit conversations. 'E's seen men pounded to just-breathing pulps at the turn of an unwanted card. 'E's seen another future 'e does not want.

But, 'e keeps telling 'imself, 'e's running 'is way out. One night at a time.

'E breathes into 'is 'ands then claps the cold from 'em. Inside 'is woollen gloves, 'is fingers sting. Inside 'is boots, 'is toes tighten. Later, when 'e sneaks back into the 'ouse, 'e'll sit on 'is bed, peel 'is skin bare and prod at the red, blistered patches, dreading Sunday morning when 'is mother will force 'im into ten inches of steaming water. First, though, 'e must stand on the corner of Raven Row, waiting on a chap who insists on calling 'im Little Rabbit.

'Go on, Little Rabbit,' 'e says. Always the same words. 'Run off. And don't come back less mine's a winner.' That's 'is routine, and Bernie knows it well. Just as 'e knows which man will appear on which street corner at which time, and which pubs 'e can loiter in front of, and which 'e ought to sneak round the back of, and which 'e shouldn't go near at all.

'Is first jaunts into the city 'ad been messier. They were explorations really, which took 'im further and further away from the little terrace 'e knew, and closer to trouble. On sweet-smelling summer nights, 'e'd stumble across lovers pinned together in doorways, and a voice would growl at 'im to 'Get lost' whilst a fist shook the threat 'ome over a shoulder. In winter mists, 'e'd find 'imself stepping across the path of an 'orse and dray and 'ave to dash blindly through the 'anging cold to escape the dark animal weight of quick-trotting 'ooves. In time, 'e grew an instinct for which streets to avoid, and when to keep 'is eyes to the ground, and who to steer clear of. But 'e'd gone against it when 'e met Garrott. Not 'cause 'e thought 'e knew better, but 'cause 'e'd seen a gristly-looking boy of about 'is own age pouring coins into the man's waiting palm, and decided that if 'e was ever going to climb 'is way out of street sweeping, 'e needed to find out where those coins 'ad come from.

Bernie 'ad always been shrewd like that – a good learner. At least that's what 'is father claims. Bernie 'ears 'im sometimes, when 'e can find an audience. 'E's sharp as a tack, my Bernie,' 'e says. And 'is friends always reply the same way, patiently: 'We don't doubt it, Perc,' they say.

But then, Bernie thinks that perhaps 'is parents 'ave never known anything about 'im.

'E 'ears stories from them now and then, about 'is smaller self – a person 'e doesn't much recognise. About 'ow 'e liked playing football in the streets with the neighbours' boys, and 'ow 'e didn't enjoy reading 'is school books, and 'ow 'e wanted to be a sweeper just like 'is daddy. Bernie remembers it differently. 'E remembers 'is parents studying 'im as though 'e were a complicated newspaper article, arms crossed over their bellies, eyes narrowed, 'eads tilting as if to stretch out their aching necks. They were searching, 'e suspected, for the evidence that would prove their assumptions. And when they couldn't find it, they retreated into their duties, disappointed again that they could not say, *'Ere's our boy, we know 'is every thought and whim.*

Truth is, Bernie will not let them know, 'cause 'e understands – 'e always 'as – that what they see when they look at 'im is only this: not enough. 'E is not one of the three or four they 'ad envisaged. 'E's just one, a part of the whole, and painful to see forever separated from the siblings who should 'ave surrounded 'im.

Percy and Josephine were relieved, 'e could tell, when 'e announced those few years back that 'e'd discovered 'e loved reading and started spending more time in 'is bedroom, living adventures safely, letter by letter. It would scuff their 'earts to know that the adventures 'e really goes on are, at times, more dangerous than those 'e or they might ever imagine.

Bernie scans the black length of Raven Row, looking for the chap who'll slope out of the dark, 'is fedora low over 'is eyes, a smoking Woodbine clamped between 'is lips. 'Little Rabbit,' 'e'll say as 'e drops a flurry of farthings into Bernie's 'and and names 'is 'orses, and Bernie will stand tall as 'e can to offset the 'umiliation of being a sweeper's son turned bookie's runner.

'E puffs up, readying 'imself for the show. 'E's good at it now. 'E's been playing the same part since that morning when 'e watched a top-hatted gentleman veer 'is motorcar over Percy's rested brush-'ead, laughing and waving as 'e snapped another man's livelihood in 'alf. Bernie'd understood right away why the man 'ad felt entitled to do it. Pride, 'e'd learnt, was a quality bound tightly to money, and so long as Percy gripped the 'andle of that brush, 'e would not be allowed to know the back-straightening pull of it. Neither would Bernie. It was up to 'im then to change things. 'E'd seen as much in the gesture 'is father made before 'e bent to retrieve 'is broken brush: it was a small thing, just a twitch of a nose, the nostrils pulsing out one shaky 'eartbeat. It was as if 'e was sniffing. Except that 'e wasn't. That twitch was the last trace of 'is anger leaving 'im, quietly, pathetically.

It was a death what went unnoticed.

Finally, Bernie spots 'is customer sauntering round the corner, 'ands in 'is pockets, eyes low. Bernie retreats a little, pressing 'imself back against a wall, where the exchange will be less obvious. 'E waits as the man flicks 'is cigarette to the ground and stamps it out, taking a bit too much enjoyment in the grinding of 'is shoe.

What *'is* parents 'oped *'e* would become, Bernie can't imagine. Surely it wouldn't 'ave been this, though. Perhaps Bernie should ask 'im 'ow 'e escaped it, the expectation. Though 'e supposes – as 'e supposes every night when 'e runs off down 'is street, boot-soles thumping the pavements, 'oping 'is parents don't 'ear the desperate rhythm of 'is departure and realise that it belongs to their own flesh and blood – that no one 'as ever 'ad so much want 'eaped on them as Bernard Percy Russell III.

'E supposes that, and 'e believes it, 'cause when 'e was small 'is mother never once told 'im a made-up story as she tucked 'im into bed. Josephine told 'im instead of 'er life, and 'is life, and 'ow the two were the same thing. Of 'ow she'd been twenty-five when she married Percy and already afraid she'd missed 'er chance. Of 'ow they'd been new to each other and excited and 'ad not spoken seriously of children when, nine weeks after their first encounter, they walked down the aisle. Of 'ow it was not until seven terrifying years later that Josephine felt the smallest blooming in 'er stomach, a watery sensation which would not dry up, and was able to tell 'er 'usband that she was growing 'im a son.

She always ended the story that same way.

'And 'ow do you know it's a son?' she'd say, putting on a gruffer voice that did not truly belong to Bernie's father. Then she'd revert to 'er normal voice. 'And I said, 'Because I can feel 'im.''

Bernie never wanted to 'ear these stories. But Josephine never asked what 'e wanted to 'ear. She just kept talking, 'er voice fading as 'e pretended to fall sleep and she continued to whisper 'er truths. Though she'd long since delivered 'im, Josephine was, and is, still full up with her Bernie.

'Hello, Little Rabbit,' Bernie's customer says now. The man grins like Bernie imagines an alley cat would, if an alley cat could do such a thing. Bernie bounces gently on the balls of 'is feet, working out that nervous tickle 'e feels all through 'im before the bet is placed.

'Who can I do you for?' Bernie asks. 'E asks it quietly, 'cause not far behind this man there's another, an 'unched pillar of darkness, approaching, and if that passing someone decides to, 'e could report Bernie to the law for running bets. Bernie curls in on 'imself, shading 'is face. 'Is customer rummages in 'is pocket for cash, oblivious.

'Mate…' Bernie mutters, flicking 'is eyes in what 'e thinks to be a subtle way, but the man doesn't catch on. 'E leans in as if 'e's deaf. 'E's too drunk for tact.

'What is it, Little Rabbit?' 'e asks, loudly, laughing. 'Little Rabbit, Little Rabbit,' 'e slurs, but 'e doesn't get to deliver the rest of 'is familiar words, 'cause that strange figure is moving fast, and 'e's almost upon them, and finally the idiot feels someone at 'is back and swings 'round, and 'Oh!' 'e goes, 'Oh!' as if that's going to 'elp when the fella lifts 'is arms above 'is 'ead and… Bernie struggles with what 'e should do. 'E could create a noise, try to distract the chap. 'E could run off, quiet, and find a bobby. 'E could do nothing at all, 'e supposes: this ain't 'is worry, after all. Bernie, though, can't sift the options through 'is 'ead quick enough to settle on one, 'cause that chap's arms are above 'is 'ead, and then they're not any more, and the next thing Bernie 'ears is the unmistakeable crack of a skull cleaving open. The man who calls 'im Little Rabbit crumples, soft suddenly, inside and out, and before Bernie can even think to move, the poor bloke is bloodying up the pavement.

There's no way 'e can survive the blow 'e's just taken to the 'ead. 'E's already not survived it. The night cold is rippling round 'is bared brain, and Bernie feels sick surging up 'is throat.

'E's never seen a dead body before. 'E squeezes 'is eyes shut.

And then, straight away, 'e 'as to open them again, 'cause they've seen it from the pub window, or they've 'eard something untoward, and the dead man's friends are coming, trundling out into the night, a big clump of them, bound firm together by fright and anger and muscle. They sound like an 'erd. They feel like an 'erd. And though Bernie needs to tell them what's just 'appened, 'e can't. 'E can only run. 'E needs to run. 'Cause they might think it was 'im.

'Is feet begin without informing 'is brain, and 'e feels 'is body being dragged along behind them. 'E knows this feeling – it means safety. Voices call after 'im. 'Oi!' they shout. 'Oi! Stop! Someone fetch the bobby!' But Bernie doesn't stop. 'E can't. 'E's running. Again. And 'e's not thinking of anyone but 'imself as 'is boot-soles thump the pavements – not 'is parents, or Garrott, or the dead man. 'E's only smiling, 'cause this is just the excuse 'e's always needed. And 'cause 'e's running again. 'E's running for Bernie. And 'e 'asn't decided yet where 'e might stop.

Matchstick Girls

Warsaw – 1943

Hidden beneath her coat, Ewa turns them in her stiff hands, feeling for each slim wooden stick. 'We'll be able to trade these, Zofia,' she whispers. 'We can trade them for food. Everyone's cold. Everyone.'

Ewa isn't sure she believes the words. Under the slumping Warsaw sky, they sound small, pressed down, stupid. But she is talking so that she doesn't have to think about what she's done.

Next to her on the pavement, Zofia shuffles around – moving slowly, measuredly, like a hunted animal – and presses her face to Ewa's side. She wants to look. Through three layers of thinning cloth, Ewa feels her sister's cheekbone slot into the cage of her ribs and slips the matches between her leg and the blanket they sit on. Not yet. There are still people on the street; people who could grow curious.

As the endless crotchet beat of passing footsteps slows to a half-note, Ewa watches the clouds slip from the sky to reveal a deeper grey beyond. Soon enough, the people and the light will disappear altogether, and Ewa will be able to reveal their prize to Zofia properly then. It will be a treat.

The sisters wrap their father's coat tighter around themselves and push into their usual corner, where the rough stone wall of a soup kitchen meets that of a tall bricked building. Ewa doesn't know what's supposed to be in there, but she does know that once every week a flock of men come and check left and right down the street before ducking inside. They each carry a package wrapped in brown paper – some long and thin as broom handles, some round and fat as cheeses – and shortly after they vanish, the music begins; hundreds of faint, tiny notes which float up from underground, like flecks of hope on the air.

Ewa pulls Zofia closer and tucks the coat around their feet. As she bends forward, she steals a quick inhalation, trying to find the smell of her father on the fabric. It's gone now. She knows it is. But she can't stop herself from seeking the soft tang of medicines laced into skin.

'Go to sleep,' she says as she straightens up again. 'Sleep until it's warmer.'

Zofia had only half woken with her sister's return, and she grumbles and closes her eyes without much fuss. Ewa listens as her breathing slows. She sleeps more and more now, slipping in and out of it with less of a fight. Sometimes, there is only the papery fluttering of her eyelids to let Ewa know she is still there, still with her.

Ewa twists her hair up and pushes it under her hat, to keep it from hardening with the cold, then rests her head against the wall. Eyes low, she watches both ways down the street. Shadows shrink and grow, but they stay close to the buildings and she can't tell which direction they come from or leave in. She is careful not to lift her head to look. She has learned to cast her eyes down; to watch the lines of legs that pass by, but never to watch the faces.

A thick layer of slushy ice covers the ground. The snow was trodden down days ago, and there has not yet been another fall to replace it. Every night now, while Zofia sleeps, Ewa sits and watches the clustering stars and wonders when the next snow will come; how she will keep Zofia warm when it does. It is getting colder all the time.

As the stillest, darkest hour of the night approaches, she brings the matches out from under their coat and starts to count them. She took them from another girl: one of the smugglers. She was no older than Zofia – five, maybe six – and Ewa hadn't known whether she was asleep or dead, but she hadn't moved when the bundle had been coaxed from her fist. She hadn't moved. Ewa stacks the matches into piles of ten near the edge of the blanket, sticking the tenth upright in the pavement slush so that it looks like a little man, watching out for the others as they repose. There are three piles, four matches left over – they might as well keep those for themselves. Ewa bundles the rest together and slides them back under her father's coat, then she takes up the first of the four and touches it to the wall beside her. She strikes it as fast as she can and, as it rasps down over the stones, it springs into life.

The heat is intense at her fingertips. Ewa had thought the flame would die of cold right away. She had prepared to pray for it, should it start to fade. But it doesn't. It keeps burning, dodging this way and that like a ballerina each time the night throws out a new, frozen gust.

Ewa leans over the flame, bringing her face to it. She feels the tip of her nose burning, and is afraid for a moment that it might melt and drip away, like a candle; but still she wants to see it close up, the way the flame shivers and fights.

It is sad that flames live for such a short time.

Somewhere in the city a dog howls, long and slow and sorrowful, then yelps into silence. The rising note wakes Zofia and she sits up, rubbing at her eyes. All is blurry, but she knows immediately that something is different – there is a new warmth, a new brightness. Usually, the buildings they sit between are grey in the moonlight. Tonight they are black, made almost invisible by that one patch of wall where an enormous dark face is looking down the street, surrounded by a halo of sunny light.

Zofia clutches her sister's arm. She recognises the flow of that neck, the rising curve of that nose. 'Look, Ewa!' she says. Her voice lurches and quivers like a kite flown in a gale. 'Look, it's Mama! It's Mama!'

Ewa swings her head around and, as she does, so their Mama swings her head around, but Zofia does not notice that they move as one. Her eyes grow wide and her mouth spreads into a huge, toothless smile: it looks more like a scream.

'See. I told you she wouldn't leave us here,' Zofia says. But as she speaks, the flame flickers and shudders and finally perishes. There is nothing before them again but a blank stretch of wall. Zofia looks to Ewa, and even in the new deeper darkness, Ewa sees the panic spill over her face. She understands what she's done then; what she has given her sister, only to take it away again. She has made a mistake.

'It's fine,' she says. 'Watch.'

She grabs for another match and strikes it against the wall. It sparks yellow with a gentle snarl. And this time, Ewa does not put her face to the flame, but uses one hand to sway it back and forth and the other to wave her fingers in front of it.

'What do you see this time?' she asks.

Zofia thinks for a moment, frowning. 'It's fish,' she answers. 'It's fish, swimming in the sea.'

'Yes, it's fish,' Ewa agrees. 'Where are they going?'

'All the way to the other side of the world.'

'Really?' Ewa says. 'All that way?'

Zofia nods, certain. And so they watch the fish swimming all the way to the other side of the world as the match burns away, extinguishing as fast and as endlessly slowly as their Father had, Ewa thinks, when those soldiers had taken their clubs to him. She shuts her eyes on the thought. But the thoughts have begun now and she cannot stop them and every time a match burns out, it is one of them, leaving her again. Their Grandmama; her entire body collapsed by a single casual aim. Their Mama, pinioned by one man and then another and then a third, before they emptied her eyes too with their final shot.

Every so often, Ewa turns to look at Zofia's illuminated face:

99

her eyes are deep and dull as dust in their sockets; her cheeks are shallow, the skin thin as the wings of an insect. On her right cheek, a long spindly bruise creeps out from under her ear and half way to her nose. She has grown so small, Ewa thinks, that she looks like an abandoned doll. And her porcelain is splitting.

As the last of their four matches burns out, Ewa says, 'Why don't you go back to sleep now? It won't be tomorrow for a long time.'

Sometimes, in the morning, a lady comes out of the soup kitchen and hands them a potato, and they sit with the hot, heavy ball between them and sniff all the smell from it before they begin to eat – a perfect half each. It lies in their stomachs then, as thick and foreign as fear once was, and the fullness hurts. Before that, though, before the sun rises, the cart goes by, and Ewa doesn't want Zofia to see the piles of naked bodies which shine sharp-white under the moon; she doesn't want her to see the stacks of jutting bones bouncing and rattling as the wheels find the ditches in the road. Some nights, Ewa sees bodies fall from the back of that cart. They land on the ground with a cracking sound, as if they are going to shatter. But they don't. They stay whole. And the driver never lifts them back on.

'No,' Zofia answers. 'I don't want to sleep. I'm going to wait for Mama to come back.'

Ewa feels under their coat for the bundle of matches. She is used to denying Zofia what she asks for. But what harm will it do, to take a few more for themselves? Just a few more. She will hold her face near them so that Zofia can see their mother again, alive in shadow, and that will send her to sleep.

But every time Zofia's eyelids begin to close, she tosses her head and forces herself to sit up straighter. She battles sleep with a stubbornness Ewa thought she had lost. And each time a match fizzles out, her face collapses like a wrecked building and Ewa has to sacrifice another.

She stops only when she hears the cart approaching.

'Quick,' she says. 'Quick, hide, or Mama won't come back again.'

With a flick of her wrists, she drapes the coat over Zofia's head and the sisters pretend to sleep as death rolls by. They used to huddle together like this for warmth, but – Ewa realises as she sneaks one eye open to watch those knotted, white people being driven away – Zofia doesn't feel warm any more. She feels like stone in her hands. Just as their mother had.

When the street falls silent once more, she returns to the matches. There is only one bundle left. She takes a deep breath and touches the first to the wall. Then she lifts her free hand, presses it to her cheek, and holds it there a moment.

'Look,' she murmurs. 'Even Mama is telling you you must go to sleep now.'

Zofia peers up at her sister. 'But if I fall asleep,' she says, 'she'll go away again.'

'No,' Ewa promises. 'She's going to watch until she's sure you're dreaming. And when you wake up, you'll be able to see her properly. And then she won't go away, not ever again.'

'Really?' The slack skin around Zofia's eyes crinkles, as though she is smiling, but her eyes remain wide and tearless, and Ewa wonders now where all her tears have gone. She used to have so many, when they were first brought here.

Ewa nods her head and hopes that she has timed her promise right. Every night this week, Zofia's breathing has grown weaker. Ewa knows that the cart will come for her soon. She won't let them take her, though. Not Zofia. Not ever. How can she? Without Zofia to care for, the woman in the soup kitchen will believe that Ewa can fight for herself. Without Zofia, she will not be gifted another potato.

Ewa tries to draw her sister closer. It is a habit she has developed lately, to tug at Zofia and measure the flexing of her limbs. She has to make sure they still move freely.

101

'Not ever,' she whispers.

'Not ever,' Zofia repeats.

Ewa nods again and presses another match-head to the wall.
'Now,' she says, 'tell me what you see.'

Live Like Wolves

Eight a.m. and already the sun was hot as grilled cheese. Francesca, packing the car for the thousandth time, was not enjoying the firm, prickling press of it as she once might have. She was irritated, perspiring, bothered. There wasn't enough room in the trunk for the cases and the few items of furniture she needed to take. She unpacked and began again, sliding the cases in lengthways this time, but it didn't help. She was going to have to leave behind something essential.

Pushing her arm across her forehead to dislodge the wilted strands of her bangs, she tried to ignore Cora, who was crying now about the lack of space for her dollies.

'But I *need* to take at least *four* of my dollies,' she whined, scuttling around her mother's feet and dragging one of those dollies face-first over the gravel driveway.

'You do not,' Fran told her daughter. 'You are seven years old, which is far too old for those silly dollies, and besides, once you see your Daddy you'll just want to play with him. Don't you miss your Daddy?'

Cora didn't answer. She forced the toe of one shoe into the dirt at the roadside, her face a furious red. 'They're not silly,' she said finally.

'You don't care about your dollies, Cora,' Fran said, gentler this time, squatting to her daughter's height. It wasn't the girl's fault. 'Look at what you're doing to Pansy.' She turned Pansy over to show Cora her newly scratched face. Immediately distraught, Cora threw herself to the ground and, licking her fingers, attempted to scrub the doll's cheeks clean; the same way Fran did her cheeks sometimes.

Unwanted for a moment, Fran considered the trunk of her ramshackle old Ford station wagon over again and decided she would abandon one of her cases. That way, she could keep the rocking chair Dylan had built. And she wouldn't need two cases, anyway; not where she was going. Dragging it free, she unzipped, removed her underwear, transferred her panties and bras to the other case, then slammed the trunk shut.

'Come on in here, Cora,' she called, moving around to open the passenger door. 'It's time to go now.'

'Go where?' Cora asked.

'You know where. To catch up to your Daddy.'

'Yes,' Cora groaned, 'but *where*?'

'We'll find that out as we go along,' Fran explained. Cora's face compacted into an expression of perfect doubt. 'It'll be an adventure.' Cora crossed her arms and legs and did not move. 'And I'm sure Pansy would like to go on an adventure, wouldn't she?'

'Really?'

'Sure. But only if you hurry up.'

Closing the door behind her, Fran noticed Cora gazing affectionately at the doll and smiled to herself. Surely Pansy was the ugliest doll ever committed to manufacture. Her coiled hair hung, limp, down to her too-broad shoulders; her glass eyes pointed in opposite directions; her lips positively sneered. And Fran knew that this was why Cora had chosen her as her favorite, and it made her proud.

'Right, are we ready?' she asked, pulling her safety belt over her chest.

'Yep,' Cora answered, cheery now. And then, quietly: 'Thank you for letting me bring Pansy.'

'That's alright, sweetheart.'

'She's my favorite, you know.'

'I know.'

'*How* do you know?'

'Because I'm your Mommy, which means I know everything,' Fran answered, winking. And Cora, not quite understanding why, giggled.

As Fran crunched the car into gear, they fell silent and listened to the metallic clunks the engine gave out when asked to move: it sounded like things were falling off of it. An angry heat swarmed Fran's body. She didn't know why they'd ever bargained for this hideous, burgundy, stick shift car – especially when they could've just stolen one. She stomped hard against the clutch, punching the wheel two-handed.

When she tried again, the car pulled away, and as they rounded the corner at the end of the street with a mechanical wheeze, Fran was surprised to find her heart beating a little faster. She forced another gear shift.

'You can do this,' she told the windscreen, but the words didn't help. She was nervous, and sad too, to be leaving the home where she'd carried her daughter; where she and Dylan had lain on the front lawn and laughed at the hugeness of her belly while someone barbequed down the street and sent the hot, sticky smell of meat gliding over them; where, earlier in her pregnancy, she had rushed from window to door to window to lock herself in because darkness had already dropped and Dylan hadn't yet come home.

She exhaled loudly. She couldn't go back. Someone else would move in shortly anyhow. Empty houses just didn't stay empty anymore. And she'd left her case on the sidewalk so as they'd notice she was gone and claim the place from her. It wasn't hers now. Not without Dylan.

On the outskirts of town they started singing. It was Cora who began it, and Fran wondered, as she clapped her hand against her thigh to her daughter's made-up tune, how the child could find any joy in a crappy car, passing by a burnt-out diner and a farm, of sorts, where five or six boney ungulates watched the occasional traffic with mournful eyes. However miserable, to Cora they were something different, something interesting.

'Can we stop and pet them?' she asked, interrupting her song.

Fran was about to protest, to say that they were in a rush, but she caught herself: already today she'd shouted at her daughter and denied the girl her home. And it was only just past nine-thirty. She could manage stroking some cows. It certainly wouldn't matter to Cora that she was acting out of guilt. She pulled over onto the roadside, kicking up a dusty tornado as her tires skidded to a stop, and they ducked out of the car, the sun hammering their backs.

At the fence, Fran lifted Cora so that she could push her feet over the second slat and reach into the field. Only one cow was willing to be touched, and Fran thanked her silently as she stood, docile, and let Cora tickle her velvet nose.

'What do you think her name is?' Cora asked.

'They don't have names, baby,' Fran answered.

'Yes they do,' the little girl said, certain. 'Daddy said that every creature in the world has a name.'

'Did he now? Well, I'm sure he's right, but how about, since she can't *tell* us her name, we decide on one for her.'

'That's an excellent idea,' Cora grinned, jumping down to pull some of the longer grass from their side of the fence. The cow munched it slowly from her tiny fist. 'I think,' she said, after a minute's deliberation, 'I'll call her Cedar'

'Cedar? After our old street?'

'Yeah. It was nice there.'

'Are you sad we have to leave?'

'Not *really* sad,' she said. 'I want to see Daddy. How far will it be?'

'I don't know, Cor,' Fran replied. 'That depends on where he is.'

Having finished her grass, Cedar opened her giant mouth into a long, deafening moo, her rope-tail flicking from side to side.

'How will we know?' Cora asked, laughing and plucking more grass for her new acquaintance.

'Well, that's the fun part,' Fran said. 'Daddy will have left us clues along the way, right, to tell us where he's gone. So what we have to do is find them.'

'But how will we know what the clues are?'

Fran stroked the tufty hair between the cow's ears. 'I don't know. We'll just have to pay real close attention, and when we see them, we'll know. Perhaps if we see another cow that's all white, just like Cedar, that will tell us which direction to go.' She said it to convince Cora the journey would be fun. Dylan's clues would be far more specific than that. He'd know Francesca would leave home and head west – he'd taught her long ago that, if lost, she was always to go west – and so he would know what she would see along the way. He would build his clues accordingly, she was sure of it. It wasn't the first time he'd disappeared. It wasn't the first time she'd had to hunt him. 'We'll look out for them together, okay? You're going to help me, aren't you?'

'Of course, Mommy.'

'Good. Right, back in the car now, please.'

'Wait!' Cora shouted, and jumping down from the fence again she ripped all the grass she could from the shaded spot she'd discovered and, clump at a time, pushed it through the fence for Cedar and her friends. Interested now, the other cows started to lollop over. Their brown patches, Fran thought as they converged, looked like a freshly drawn map.

Eighty miles further west than Fran had ever ventured and Cora had slept and woken again. Small-eyed, she dangled her head over her safety belt, forehead almost touching the window, and watched the white lines roll by. Fran wondered how much of the changing landscape she was taking in. Already the sandy fields were growing greener, fatter. The mountains were creeping nearer with every passing town. And the sky... Fran had never seen anything like it. She'd existed inside a hundred-mile perimeter her entire life. But she could understand now why Dylan should want to come this way, towards skies which were bigger than those at home; which hung, like bedsheets on a clothesline, inches from the tree tops.

It was all very simple, now.

Perhaps, she thought, if they went far enough, they'd circle round and be able to see the Statue of Liberty. She must be a real sight. Though her head had come off years back, Fran knew people still went to visit her, to marvel at her. But, no. 'He always wanted to go to the mountains,' she breathed.

'What?' Cora turned to face her mother, rubbing one stubborn eye. She was desperate to stay awake, to see her Daddy's first clue. She was hoping it would be a cow, like her Mom had said.

'Nothing, baby. I was just talking to myself. Did I wake you?'

'Did you see a clue yet?'

'Not yet.'

'Good.'

'Go back to sleep, Cora,' Fran said. 'There won't be anything to see for a good long while.'

And there wasn't, which got Fran to worrying. She'd been imagining directions spray-painted on the side of a barn, or branches ripped from trees and arranged into letters on the roadside. But perhaps her thinking was too obvious. Perhaps she'd missed a hundred, subtler, signs already. 'He always wanted to go live with the wolves,' she whispered. Hadn't he always said that to Cora, sitting in front of her highchair and howling while he fed her? *We can go live like wolves,* he'd say, *and eat fish from the rivers, and share our supper with the birds and the rabbits and the badgers.* He'd act out each animal then, flapping and squawking or snuffling along the kitchen floor, nose down, and Cora would laugh and laugh at her 'silly Daddy', and Francesca loved him in those moments.

Now, she was trying to persuade herself to hate him.

He'd made things so difficult for her, disappearing like that. Sure, he'd had the decency to leave behind the wagon and the cash. But what use was cash in finding a person? In finding a life? She sneaked a look at Cora – fast asleep again. *The world just isn't shaped like it used to be, Fran,* he'd say, when he was feeling dark. *We need to find a new shape; a better shape.* And of course she'd asked what that shape should look like, but he couldn't put it into words for her. So all she could think of were the wolves.

The wolves, she decided, would be her signs.

Passing by a bundle of homes as dusk lazed in, Cora screeched and Francesca slammed on the brakes, lightly head-butting the steering wheel as the car bumped and stalled.

'Jesus Christ, Cora,' she fumed, 'what the hell is wrong with you?'

'I'm sorry,' Cora began, filling up, her lower lip wobbling.

'No. Don't you dare cry!' Fran unclipped her belt and spun around to grab her daughter by the shoulders. 'You tell me right now why you almost made me kill us.' Spots of her saliva landed on Cora's face and the little girl grimaced.

'I saw one of Daddy's clues,' she said quietly, eyes down. In her lap, she twisted Pansy's arm round and round in a way no human could tolerate. The arm remained willfully intact.

Francesca fell back against her seat and closed her eyes. She felt she was going to vomit. One of his clues, and she'd almost missed it with her tiredness and bad thoughts. Dylan would never forgive her such an oversight. He never had been a forgiving man.

When they'd first been married, Fran had made the mistake of teasing him about the bramble leaf of thinning hair around his crown, and Dylan had answered her joke with six days of silence. She'd had to learn fast that Dylan wasn't like any other man she'd known.

Pushing her arm over her forehead, she opened her eyes again. Cora hadn't moved.

'I'm sorry, baby. Mommy's sorry, okay? I'm just tired. It isn't your fault.'

Cora nodded solemnly, eyes still cast down.

'What did you see, Cora?'

'A sign,' she said.

'I know a sign,' Fran snapped again. 'What kind of sign? What was it?'

'It was a sign,' Cora shouted back at her mother, head springing up. 'A sign. Back there by those trailers.'

Fran jammed the car into reverse and, sticking her head over her shoulder, backed crazily down the road, sending the car swinging this way and that like a fish on the sand.

'There. There,' Cora shouted, pointing, as they reached the place. She bounced in her seat. 'See, I knew it was there. I sawed it.'

'Saw what?' Fran could see nothing much: a few wooden shacks; nine or ten dirty trailers; a wire fence, split open in places, bending around the lot. Beyond the fence, a couple kids, dressed in only their underwear, were setting something alight. There was nothing of her husband here.

'The writing, Mommy!'

Fran squinted her bleary, driving eyes. Carved into the dust on the side of one of the trailers were the words, *Congratulations on your Anniversary, Renate and Oswald.*

'Do you see it, Mommy?'

'I do, baby. But I don't understand.'

'Look at the big letters,' Cora said. 'They spell my name!'

Fran read it again. 'So they do,' she said, stroking her daughter's copper hair. 'You were clever to spot that, Cora. Very clever indeed.'

Francesca held her breath as she knocked on the trailer door. A deep voice hollered from within. 'One minute, stranger.' Fran couldn't decide whether it was male or female. Turning, she checked Cora was still in the car, door locked like she'd told her. Cora waved at her, smiling. Poor girl. All Fran had done to her this last six months, and she still smiled so willingly. Fran was ashamed of herself: ashamed that she'd shown Cora her anger; ashamed that she was making her chase her Daddy across the country. Though the evening was still throbbing with heat, she felt as though someone had poured a bucket of ice down her back.

'What can I do for you, honey?'

The woman at the door stood at a stringy six-feet-something, her shoulders leaping away from her body as if scared. In her right hand, an enormous wooden spoon. Hanging from her left, a baseball bat.

Fran eyed the bat.

'Oh, sorry.' The woman shrugged and threw the bat onto a chair behind her. 'Can't be too careful.'

Fran still wasn't speaking.

'Although, I don't think a skinny miss like you can do me much harm. Unless you've a pistol hidden in there somewhere.' She nodded towards the car. 'You want to come in?'

'No,' Fran said. 'No, thank you, I…'

'You know where you're headed, honey?'

'No… Sort of. I… was wondering if you've seen a man pass this way?'

'Haven't seen any man anywhere near recent enough,' the woman replied, laughing. 'When're we talking?'

'Six months past. He's…' But she didn't how to describe him, her husband – the man she'd chosen to father her child; the man she'd promised her forever to. Dylan wasn't especially anything. Not short, not fair, not slim, not handsome. She couldn't show this woman with simple words how unexpectedly he plunged into his moods, or how scared he was of himself, or why he ran. It was perhaps only Fran who could see – in the rippling tension about his jaw, in the fractional lift of his shoulders – when Dylan was preparing to run. 'He's lost,' she concluded.

The woman shook her head. 'No one comes to mind,' she said. 'Not so far as I remember. Is there anything else I can help you with? Why not come in and have some lunch?'

'That's kind,' Fran answered. 'Thank you, but we need to get on.'

'We?'

'My daughter. I'm taking her to see her father.'

'You have a long way to go?'

'I don't know,' Fran sighed. 'I just don't know. I wish I did, but I don't, and… He's supposed to be leaving me clues.'

'Clues?' the woman asked, stepping down from her trailer to take Fran by the arm now – it seemed she was going to keel right over. 'What sort of clues?'

'Well,' Fran explained, her face flushing, 'on the side of your trailer, the words, the congratulations… Do you know who wrote that?'

'One of the kids. For their grandparents.'

'Oh, okay, we just thought, my daughter and me. We just thought…'

Fran released the sentence and let it float away. She looked up at those clean, fresh clouds as though she could see it leaving her; disappearing, like a promise. The trailer shone silver against the sun, and Fran had to raise a hand to shield her eyes. She felt close to fainting. She'd never been this far from home, never once, and

Dylan had made it sound so exciting. They could go live like wolves, just like that. But she didn't feel like a wolf. Wolves were proud and strong and fearless, and she was not. She was just Francesca. And she didn't know how far across the country it was possible to tow her daughter.

'We thought it might be him,' she concluded.

Fran was careful to smile as she bent back into the car.

'Was it him, Mommy?' Cora burbled. 'Has he been here?'

'Well, I'm not sure,' Fran explained, 'but that lady there said a young man stopped by a few months back and had some lunch with her before moving on. It could have been Daddy, Cora.'

'Really?'

'Really.'

As she pulled her belt back across her pounding chest, Fran saw the woman hobbling from her trailer, a plastic bag in hand. She seemed to need a stick to walk on, but she didn't have one. Grasping the cross around her neck, Fran prayed she wouldn't say anything to give away her lies. They were only small lies, necessary ones, to keep Cora interested a while longer. Fran didn't deserve to be found out. They'd find a clue sooner or later, a real one, and everything would be right then. Everything would be just fine once they found Dylan.

Fran unwound the window and, facing straight ahead, waited. Hoped.

'Something for the road,' the woman said, lifting the bag into the car.

Turning to meet her eye, Fran caught a flicker of the secret sadness there. 'Thank you,' she whispered and, hanging her hand out the window, she grasped the woman's fingers. For a fraction of a second they pressed their palms together, held on tight. But they couldn't stay that way, and grudgingly Fran released her.

'Good luck,' the woman said, smiling without showing her teeth. 'I'm sure you'll find him.' And without waiting for

Francesca to reply, she stepped back towards her trailer, shouting, 'You cause that fire to spread, Billy, and I'll kill you, I really will,' as she walked. Billy lifted his head and laughed nastily. And then the woman was gone, and Fran was alone once more with her daughter: her good, clever daughter.

She restarted the engine. 'Right. Are we ready?' she asked, grinning like a clown.

'Ready,' Cora confirmed.

'You know we're going to have to practice our howls before we get there, right?'

'Our howls?'

'Sure,' Fran answered, and lifting her chin to the sky, she rounded her lips and let out her best 'aaoooowww.'

'Like the wolves?' Cora asked.

'That's right,' she said. 'Just like the wolves. We're going to live like wolves.'

'Are you sure, Mommy? Which way did he go? Which way did Daddy go?'

Fran breathed deep through her nose. It was necessary, the lie. And besides, she wanted to believe it, too. She would not abandon him now. 'Just the way we're going, baby,' she said. 'Just the way we're going.'

Hunting Shishe

She is woken by a swelling panic. It arrives through the gap beneath her bedroom door, in the shape of a phrase maybe, or an exclamation, which has begun far away and travelled fast; as fast as the echoes can carry it through the lengths of that draughty house. Staff members passing in the service corridors will have nodded, she knows, and pressed their lips together, trying not to speak the words, but they are heard anyway. They are whispered by the dust. Teacups, rattling in their saucers, seem to chink them out. Doors slam to their rhythm. They become tangible – as the disastrous always does – on the air itself.

'She's gone!' That's what they say. 'She's gone!'

And somehow, without needing to be told, Roanne knows that they mean Shishe. Shishe is missing.

In one smooth movement, she rises from bed and thrusts on a pair of old, brown working boots, the first pink fragments of day breaching the curtains to sting her eyes. The kitchen, she decides. The cook will know what's happening. And, downstairs, she does not pause to hear her suspicions confirmed, but flies through the narrow galley, part-blinded by the steam, ankles twisting in her oversized boots, her hair rippling behind her like loose reins.

'Shishe?' she calls.

'Yes!' the cook answers, waving one arm above her head so that the muscle trembles. 'How did you…'

But Roanne does not slow. Still heavy-eyed, she staggers down the steps from the kitchen, rights herself, then skids over the gravel courtyard, racing into the fresh glare of the morning. She

115

makes for the stables, imagining she might find her brother tangled in tack, attempting to saddle up a horse for the chase. In moments, she will rush in and beg him to let her go, too. She has to help. She has to find Shishe. But the stables are empty of people: just the five horses stand within, silent, bumping their bodies against the stall walls in an attempt to find the hot comfort of their instinct in another's rump or flank. They are scared. Likely, Shishe passed through this way. Perhaps that's why Hamilton didn't ride one of them out, Roanne thinks. It does not occur to her that you cannot seek a predator with a weaker animal until she is running out through the Menagerie's main gates, her white nightdress billowing in the cold-edged breeze, her bare-skinned feet slapping noisily inside those untied boots. And it is too late then to consider what an unchallenging prey animal she herself is. She is already part of the hunt.

Even before she reaches the end of the driveway, though, she is forced to adjust her stride. She is breathless. She has not run anywhere since the urgency of childhood. She slows slightly and, as she veers left to enter the acres of woodland which surround the property, permits herself one quick glance at the house; the black iron sign above the gate which reads *Hamilton Prade's Menagerie*; the peaked roofs of the enclosures. She does not want to look back. She does not want to see it. She pushes on, the way Shishe would, leaving all the evidence of her existence behind her.

As the morning plumps into day, Roanne climbs to the highest point of the immediate land. Here, the wind blows cleaner and more determined before dipping down into the valley. She wraps her arms around her middle and, bracing her body against a shiver, scans the jagged territory below, her eyes following the river's trickle into nothingness.

Somewhere down there, Old Clyde – the Prade's warden for

over forty years now – will be scrutinising the earth for tracks. He remains capable, despite his age. He knows his animals. Roanne hopes, though, that he is not the first to discover Shishe; she hopes, for his sake, that it is not he who will have to risk shooting at her. A bad aim would break his heart. Still, he will perform his duties perfectly. She knows that. He will train his eyes downwards and trudge every root of this countryside, and he will not lift his head again until Shishe is found.

And Roanne will do the same, she determines, as she turns and marches recklessly into the rest of her search. She will do the same.

Hamilton is moving differently. Knees bent deep, feet feeling out each careful step, gun held far out in front of him, he steals about like a thief, hoping against a discovery. Where there are natural hollows to hide in, Hamilton lingers for long minutes. When he wanders as far as the treeline, he drops sharply away from the prospect of exposure. He does not care, the way Roanne will, if Shishe is lost. He will not mourn the animal if, unaccustomed now to the size of the world outside her cage, she has stumbled from a high ledge and fallen to her death. He can purchase another tiger. He is out here, searching, only because it is what his father would have done. The first Hamilton Prade would not have allowed any creature to escape his ownership. The second Hamilton Prade, though, is nervous: no jailer would want to encounter his prisoner outside of the prison.

The scuffling of wings somewhere nearby startles him and Hamilton grips the neck of his gun tighter, swinging it left and right in wild arcs.

'Who's there?' he gasps. 'What's there?'

But he can see nothing. Perhaps it is only the ghost of his father, reminding him that he must not stop. He must never stop.

117

Though she is high above him, though she has not yet seen any sign of him, Roanne has no doubt that her brother is terrified of the hot breath, the bristling whiskers hidden amongst the trees. Hamilton, after all, is afraid of so much. Roanne is not afraid, though, as she searches out that familiar flash of warm orange fur, that moving, black lightning stripe, that low-in-the-throat grumbling. Somewhere, soft, strong paws are marking their own path for the first time in a lifetime.

It has always troubled her that they make their living by locking up souls. In her earliest memories, she wonders why the Prade's should have to own a zoo and not a fairground or a labyrinth or any of those other fun, sprawling venues children dream of. Then, as now, she would stalk between the enclosures, trying to send telepathic messages to the animals. *Where is your country?* she would think to them. Or, *Please don't be sad.* She didn't know whether they were sad or not, but she suspected it of them all.

All, that was, except Shishe. Though she alone lacked a mate, Shishe was and is too proud to be sad. When she bares the sharp conoids of her canines, she does so slowly enough to demonstrate that you should not think yourself worth the effort. When she shoots her freckled lime stare at you, her eyes are coloured with defiance.

In her early twenties, Roanne had practised that stare in the mirror. Once, sitting in dark rain near the giraffe enclosure, she had used it to keep a date's hand from sneaking further under her skirt. She has not always had Shishe's strength, though. There have been other hands she has not stopped.

Roanne follows some instinct down to the river. There, settling on a wide, level stone, she dips a hand into the flow. Despite the mild weather, the water is icy and her skin grows red and numb immediately but she does not lift her arm out. She used to do this as a child, sitting amongst the flamingos and holding a hand or a foot under the lake's surface until the sensation in all four extremities disappeared. It made her feel invisible. And if Shishe could think as people do, Roanne supposes, she would be wishing for invisibility now.

What would it make of her, though, to think as a human would? Surely, it would enervate her, to know that she is beautiful and terrifying and stronger than any man. Roanne plunges her other hand into the water and stretches out her neck. No, an animal could not tolerate such arrogance.

Shishe has long been her favourite. When sleep eludes her – and it does so more and more of late – she pulls on her old leather boots and wanders through the Menagerie, and it is always to Shishe's enclosure that she goes last. At the bars of Shishe's prison, she sits down and talks, her voice a tiny thing that goes pinballing around between the planets. And when no one is looking at her, it is the tigress Roanne turns to, and each growl or rumble or huff Shishe releases is a question to which Roanne tries, again and again, to find an answer; just a word or a sentence that would reveal, satisfactorily, what is wrong. The only word she could utter honestly is *nothing*. Nothing is wrong. Her entire life, to date, has revolved around the evasion of any sort of feeling.

She pulls her hands from the river and leans back to remove her boots. She has liberated only one foot when Hamilton hisses at her from some hidden place.

'Ro! What are you doing?'

She glances about herself, searching him. She does not say his name to prompt him to speak again. Lately, she has been refusing these little inanities, but Hamilton is either ignorant of or choosing to ignore her apathy.

'She'll see you.'

Roanne resumes unlacing her boots. When she responds, it is at her usual volume; perhaps slightly louder. 'What if she does?'

'She'll tear you apart.'

Roanne drops her boot, enjoying the empty thud of its landing, the way the valley walls repeat it twice over, like a heartbeat.

'And won't that be dramatic,' she answers.

There would be no pain if Shishe took an arm or a leg, she is sure of that much. The impact, the tearing, the blood loss – they would hurl her body into shock. The pain would come much later, when she was bandaged into her new, lighter body and forced to lie still for days, waiting on the doctor's next visit. In that particular daydream, it is her left arm she surrenders to Shishe's teeth; her left arm which is carried away into Scotland and consumed to give Shishe the energy to clamber towards the country's tip. Roanne enjoys some small part of that idea – her own flesh, fuelling a three-hundred-and-fifty pound Bengal tigress as she runs into the knowledge that, yes, she was built for this exertion, this space, this endless movement.

It sometimes seems to Roanne that she was built for nothing more than imagining; that she is composed only of reveries and resolutions. The thought saddens her.

'Come here, Ro. Quick!'

Roanne doesn't need to see her brother to know that he is beckoning as he speaks. Probably, he is biting his lip, too; a sign of frustration which so often appears when he is not being listened to. Or adored. Or allowed into her bedroom.

'Do you remember,' she begins, sending her words over her shoulder now that she has located, roughly, his whereabouts, 'how Daddy used to tell us that animals were for doing and people were for thinking?'

Hamilton does not like the tone of her voice. It is looser than usual, unravelled. It is the voice she speaks to Shishe with. Hamilton recognises it from all those times he has stood behind the enclosure and listened to her, pouring her fears into a tiger's dreams. It is not the voice she uses to speak to him. A voice, he supposes, cannot be contained.

'Of course,' Hamilton answers.

'Well, I've changed my mind about that.' She stands and turns towards the rock Hamilton must be crouched behind. 'Stand up, will you?'

Hamilton's head pokes slowly into view. His hair is flattened to his scalp in places, and Roanne thinks he looks like a mental patient, newly released. Although, perhaps she appears just as wild to him, her nightdress rippling around her body like a white flag, her dark hair beating the ashen sky. She might look like a mad woman, having fled her home only to forget what it is she is seeking. And that, really, is how she feels. And that is why she needs to walk, anywhere, everywhere.

'I'll see you back at the house,' she says, striding away.

The notion that Hamilton will not follow her is a new and beautiful one. And yet he cannot. She knows it. He is too scared. But she is not afraid: not of Shishe; not of having her arm ripped off; not even, in this moment, of feeling. Because surely the bad things, too, must be felt. That is what her existence – always at the centre of everything in that big sprawling house, always waited on, always accommodated – has failed to teach her.

When her feet find grass again, she hitches up her nightdress to step more freely. The earth, holding onto memories of the previous night's cold, sends a tingling through her skin and she smiles. She smiles and smiles and, once she is on level ground, she starts to run. She does not look back to the place by the river where her boots sit – one upright, the other tipped onto its side, the laces flailing in the breeze as though the person who once wore them has vanished. She does not look back. She is gone.

Roanne and Hamilton Prade were homeschooled, by a succession of exhausted tutors who tried and failed to instil in the children some, any, sense of fun. The Prade children, however, had not been raised for fun. They found those few contemporaries they did encounter to be trivial in their thoughts, infantile in their behaviour. They despised the enforced frivolity of their existence. And so, when their father's wine-bulged heart stopped one night and his body was abandoned to the flagstones of his library floor, they knew exactly how to behave: they had a purpose now. They stood in proud black at their father's graveside as he was lowered in next to their mother. They thanked their guests and well-wishers with dry eyes. And when the funeral was over, they completed their schoolwork to their usual exceptional standards. They were the mirrors of their parents, the truest reflection of their upbringing.

'I'll be in charge now,' Hamilton informed his sister quietly, as they ascended the stairs to their bedrooms that night. 'It makes sense. I'm the oldest.'

'Old Clyde is the oldest,' Roanne replied.

'He isn't a Prade, though. I'm the only Prade man left.' Hamilton – fifteen, skinny, not at all forceful, then – puffed himself up as he spoke. He was not the figure his father had been. He knew that. But he might be, given time. He might learn to stand in a room as though his very presence in it was keeping the walls erect. He might develop a belly rounded by rich food. And he might be able, then, to command people as his father had.

Hamilton pushed open his bedroom door and glanced through at the smooth white stretch of his bedsheets. He would begin practising right away. 'Come on,' he said.

And Roanne – thirteen and desperate – understood instantly what he wanted. She did not make a sound as she stepped past him through the door. She was almost willing, that once.

She happens across a narrow stream and slows to a stroll, trusting the sound of the water to silence her thoughts. The afternoon is growing heavy and she has almost given up hope of finding Shishe. She is walking now solely for the enjoyment of it. She picks over the shallower spots, relishing the momentary divergence of water around her ankles. It is only a few inches deep, but it has a strong pull and she wishes she had a little paper boat – the kind her father used to fold for her when she was a girl – to set sail on it.

Even then, she had been obsessed with the idea of freedom.

She used to tell the animals about it. When she made her sleepless midnight rounds, she would stop to watch the giant tortoises haul themselves up and down the grassy mound of their home and she would whisper to them: 'Wouldn't you like to slide out of that shell? Wouldn't you be happier, carrying nothing on your back?'

On the opposite side of the stream, she pauses to look back down the valley, to estimate how far she has come, to see whether Hamilton or Clyde are anywhere near. Turning, though, she finds that she has walked her way into a web of trees. Rows of wide trunks bed themselves into the earth before rising, tapering as they go, towards the clouds. Where there should be a band of blue sky, there is only the canopy the leaves have knitted, a hundred shades of green, and the buttery glow of the sun, reaching through their gentle stitching.

It is getting late. If she is to continue following this incline, she should perhaps return to the stream for water. But she has nothing to carry it in, and she doesn't feel thirsty yet, and it would be cautious to go back, and she has already promised herself that today will not be about caution. Today is about every time she has not laughed, or jumped, or run. Today is about every time she has not unlocked a cage door.

She spins around and runs a little way up the mountain, her feet slipping on dropped pine needles and crawling moss, her arms flapping about to keep her upright. Almost immediately, her breath sticks in her throat and she stops, laughing at herself, at how weak she is. Shishe would cover the same ground like a shadow, flowing over the roughness as though it were flat as glass. She steadies her breathing, sucking air in fast through flared nostrils. She holds out her arms to let the breeze into her nightdress. And when her heart finally rediscovers its rhythm, she realises that it is not one set of lungs she can hear, inhaling and exhaling, but two.

Shishe is at her back.

Roanne tries to recall everything her father taught her about the animals. But her father had always been teaching, had always had a book in hand, had always needed to test and retest his theories, and she doesn't know whether she should be standing still and waiting for the tigress to lose interest, or making herself appear larger so that the animal feels threatened, or scrambling up the nearest tree trunk in the feeble hope that she will not be pursued. So she opts to do the brave thing. As quietly as possible, she shifts her feet like clock hands, passing one hour then pausing before approaching the next. She rotates through six, slow, imaginary hours, until she is facing Shishe, who stands in the path ahead, maybe five yards distant, her head hanging down below her shoulders so that she considers Roanne through fans of white lashes, her nose twitching, her whiskers trembling.

Roanne counts the black lines which flame outwards from Shishe's eyes, like flicks from a mascara brush. She breathes in the hot, muscular smell of her. And then she breathes out. She has spoken to this animal a thousand times. Perhaps she should do so again, to remind Shishe of her voice. She utters the first words that ripple towards her tongue.

'It's about not making a mistake, girl. That's what it's always been about – do you see?' Roanne isn't sure what exactly it is she's talking about, but she suspects that if she just keeps going, it might become clearer. She lowers herself gradually downwards until she is kneeling. 'But today, today is for you. Do you like it out here? Hmm? There's so much to see…'

Shishe takes two steps forward, legs bending out like a pair of brackets as each paw accepts her weight. Then she, too, sits.

'Or perhaps not,' Roanne continues, her voice graduating from a whisper to her normal tone. 'Perhaps, when you live in a cage for so long, you forget how to look, how to see. Perhaps all this choice is too much.'

The tigress listens silently, tilting her head now and then, thinning her eyes, sweeping her tail. She lifts a paw and licks an itch away with one rasp of her tongue.

'I wish you could answer me, girl.'

It is indisputable, to Roanne's mind, that Shishe will move up the country now, towards the hush of the mountains. There is nothing here for her but the click and glare of cameras, uninvited looks, grasping hands; nothing but noise and fear. Of course she will choose escape. She'll choose long, swaying summers, and waste them slinking from one shaded spot to the next or splashing into shallowing streams. She'll choose the crisp relief of autumn. She'll choose the first crack of frost beneath her paws, and the revolving sight of the moon, and the starvation of the winter months. She'll choose wounds that will be tended only by her own saliva, and shivering into sleep in a country she should never have known, and, eventually, she will begin to limp badly on her front left leg and she'll fail in one hunting expedition, then two. She will choose, after that, to feel her bones start to protrude through her skin and her stripes dip into the gaps between her ribs. But they will be her choices – hers and hers alone. And she will honour them.

What Roanne can't decide is whether or not she should choose to choose with her.

Tiring of their conversation, the tigress pushes herself back up onto all four paws. Roanne remains still, ensuring that eye contact is not broken. Prey, she supposes, does not often make eye contact with the predator, and the action might just set her apart. As Shishe paces nearer, though, she can't keep her heart from pulsing harder against her chest. She imagines it becoming audible to the tigress, visible even – soft and edible as a piece of fruit. She tries to think it calm, but the effort doesn't help. Its rate increases with every inch Shishe covers. Roanne opens her mouth, thinking she might make one last appeal, but she does not have chance to select her words before Shishe is upon her, pushing her enormous head against Roanne's shoulder, then circling all the way round the kneeling woman, scrubbing her face, her shoulder, her ribcage, her flank against Roanne's breath-held fright. Shishe's throat issues a gentle grumble. Her tail traces a line along Roanne's cheek. Then, finally, her tail tip whips away and Roanne is naked of her again: naked but for that scent, so strong, so sour, that it settles on her – like someone else's jacket, draped over you after you've dropped into sleep.

'Shi –' she begins, but she realises immediately that this is not the animal's name. The name the tigress gives herself is a secret she will never share.

'Good luck,' Roanne whispers instead as she watches Shishe walk away, her shoulders rolling, her hips dipping languidly left and right, her paws spreading so wide and flat over the earth that it seems she is trying to press herself into it.

Roanne remains where she sits until Shishe is only a diminishing line of paw prints and the recollection of a black tail tip, disappearing amongst the trees. What would Hamilton say to that confrontation? She knows to the letter. Get after her, he'd say. Get after her and bring her back. And she can picture him so clearly – taking off along the trail Shishe has left, his head snapping frantically this way and that, his breath stalling as he shouts abuse at her and Old Clyde – that she wonders for a moment if it is a memory. And though Shishe has never escaped before, perhaps, in some ways, it is. She stands and brushes down her nightdress. Perhaps she has wasted her whole life just watching that man rush from one fit of anger to another.

But there is no perhaps about it. It is definite. And that is why it is so easy now to choose a new direction. That is why she is able to follow Shishe's lead and, turning, walk away. Just that – walk away. The bravest thing a person could do.

Ten days later, the search team Hamilton employs finds Roanne's nightdress, tangled in some low reaching branches and spectacularly torn, as though by the swipe of four inch claws. They draw their conclusions, and the household staff draw theirs, and eventually somebody goes to the newspapers with the story. It is not long then before there is rumour, not only of a three-hundred-and-fifty pound Bengal tigress who roams the borderlands, hunting her heritage, but of a woman, or the ghost of a woman, who is brave enough to negotiate the mountains with her.

Hamilton considers fighting these stories. He writes columns of his own for the newspapers to print, dispelling the mounting myths and begging Roanne, if she reads them, to come home. But he cannot find the right words, and the articles never appear. Any strength he had possessed leaked out of him the day she and Shishe left.

As the years turn, he buys up more land, orders bigger enclosures built, hires two more wardens to assist Old Clyde, and then he retreats to their father's library, where he watches the days seep away over the tops of unread pages.

Roanne does not offer him any comfort. If she is still alive, she does not return to the house. She does not post a letter. Still, Hamilton imagines her constantly, waking early and strolling alone along a cold shore, her gloved hands thrust into the pockets of a sand-length coat; or sitting to tea in a garden overgrown with some variety of lacing, violet bud, a sunhat painting crisscross patterns over her cheeks; or raising children in an unknown European city, a new language on her tongue as she walks tree-lined pavements. He never imagines that she will come back. He is more intelligent than that. But he can hope for Shishe. He can hope that some impulse will draw her back towards what she once knew. And he does, in his most selfish moments.

On good days, though, when he wakes to a clear sky and eats a large breakfast and feels fleetingly generous, Hamilton is sure to think Shishe away from this place. Though she is no doubt nothing more now than a collection of clean, strong bones, he is sure, when he tells her story, to leave the tigress where Roanne would have left her – in the mountains, easy and free and walking away, always walking away, towards nothing but herself.

The Dancing Man

He moved with all the strength and intent of an eagle. A few steps in one direction then he would tilt his head, drop a shoulder, and swoop off in another, circling like a hunter. His every movement was majestic; imposing; designed, it seemed, by nature. There was no music playing, but then, he didn't need any. He danced to the sigh of the wind, moving as easily as a feather caught on its frozen currents. Beyond him, the station's opposite platform was blanched by dropping snow.

As he completed his first rotation, Kayleigh lifted her hands to clap. Then, remembering the rest of his reluctant audience, she pushed them through her hair and dropped them back into her lap. The dancing man spun past and began marking the same path again, his shoes dipping into the dents he'd already made in the snow. He wasn't stopping yet, and Kayleigh was glad. She leaned back against the hard slats of the bench and watched him rise onto the balls of his feet, twirl around, then bending his knees, float away from her.

This, she thought, was how she would learn to dance; sitting still, her eyes fixed on a stranger's feet. She'd always wanted to be able to dance.

Scanning the platform, she wondered why nobody else was watching him. There was no other movement here, on a railway station the snow had stopped two hours earlier, but the gentle parade of grey clouds across the steely sky and the occasional flapping of squabbling pigeons. His footsteps were the only thing worth looking at.

The other three remaining passengers stared down at the bare ground beneath the benches, curling in on themselves like the petals of sleeping flowers. It was obvious, from their hunched bodies, their set faces, that they were still hoping the train would appear. Kayleigh wasn't. It seemed to her that the whole world had creaked and stalled, and though she knew that failing to reach the office today would mean facing her last warning, there was a familiar kind of pleasure in being where she should not be.

She pushed her blueing hands into the opposite arms of her coat and tucked up her legs, making herself smaller to preserve some heat: still slight in her late twenties, she looked like a child in her mother's clothes. She stomped her feet against the bench, making it twang. At the far end, a white-whiskered man turned in her direction to frown and mumble, and Kayleigh fought the urge to laugh. Beneath his jacket, a shirt and tie were closed around his neck. Perhaps he was going to be late for work, too. Kayleigh couldn't make herself care. She didn't want to go to work, anyway. She wanted to stay outside, cocooned inside her coat, and watch the snow drop around her. She wanted to stick her tongue out to catch the flakes. Pushing her tongue against her teeth, however, she found that it would go no further.

The dancing had started with a tapping foot – an attempt to stay warm, probably. But it had grown, slowly, into what Kayleigh thought might be a tango. Or a waltz. Without music, or a partner, the shapes were difficult to discern. But he seemed to have been circling the platform forever now, this stranger in a black suit and a red scarf; his feet tracing definite lines and his body billowing after them, like a balloon on a weighted string. It was only persuading her that she was right not to go in search of a taxi.

Despite her secret pleasure, Kayleigh didn't set herself apart from the other people on the platform. When they averted their eyes or slid down the benches away from him, she said nothing.

When the woman furthest from her hurled a clump of indecipherable words at him, hard as cricket balls, she did not stand to dance with him.

Instead, she went to get herself a coffee from the machine and chose a different seat when she came back.

She knew what they were thinking. And as her limbs grew colder and the sky thickened, she conceded that they might be right. He might be mad. She didn't want to get too close. But she couldn't stop herself from looking still, following the blood-like trickle of his scarf against the sky, counting the even *one two three* of his feet. The first step held the emphasis – it had purpose, direction. The second and third were tentative, like words you wished you'd spoken louder. Was that a waltz? Whatever it was, it was beautiful: the black suit and coat, the red scarf, the snow under his shiny black lace-ups. He looked like a man from another time.

She almost smiled. But she didn't want the others coupling her with this man. Two wasn't a big enough number – that's what Leah in the next office always told her over lunch, angling her tiny hand so that her wedding ring shone under the fluorescent lighting. And Kayleigh believed her. It was possible that her workmates were the only reason she hadn't quit her job earlier – because there were enough of them to ensure that someone was always going out to eat, or to a bar, or to the theatre. It didn't matter if they were general invitations or not, Kayleigh had found that she could wriggle her way into plans as easily as she would wriggle into a black dress and a pair of heels. And anything was preferable to a night in, alone, in a flat someone else had decorated.

She checked her watch. Nearly an hour late. She shoved the sleeve of her coat back over the shiny clock-face.

Her job would kill her eventually. It would stretch her nerves until they sagged in exhaustion. It would penetrate her mind and

131

turn her most riotous dreams into filing cabinet thoughts. Every new ambition would sink into the anticipation of a week off here, a day off there; simple hours to waste in dread at the prospect of returning to the same building, the same desk, the same chair, the same computer, the same cyclical conversation.

This man had the right idea. His feet barely grazed the snow as he floated to the edge of the platform, soared past the drop, and spun back towards safer ground. He didn't have a single worry. He was dancing. In this frowning, crouching, snow-stilled city, he was dancing.

The tannoy crackled, whispered, then clicked off again. Whatever news it had intended to impart must have changed. Kayleigh slumped lower into the fur-lining of her coat. Nothing could be relied upon once the snow fell. Everyone knew that. She could feel heads turning towards the speaker, hear the other passengers huffing, as though they believed that hating the device enough would force it into communication.

Kayleigh did not mirror their movement. She wasn't interested now in words. She had long since learned the danger of them.

She had only once declared – aged thirteen, maybe fourteen – that she wanted to be an architect. What it was that had inspired her, she couldn't remember. It was likely something fleeting: she had been a fleeting sort of teenager, gliding almost daily from one thought, one love, one hope, one gripe, to a sharply contradictory other. The sight of a glamorous actress with a drawing board would have been enough. Kayleigh wanted to be anything she wasn't. But – for some reason she still hadn't uncovered – when she had mentioned her architectural ambitions, they had stuck. She had set herself on a track that led straight from a before-bed idea in her early teens to a pencil skirt, a new city, and a forty-hour-a-week contract. And she hadn't once bothered trying to get off it.

Catching her eye as he swung by, the dancing man smiled at

Kayleigh; a shy, tight-lipped movement which persuaded her that, despite his skill, he wasn't completely comfortable with his performance either. Why do it then? Kayleigh was about to ask, but he spoke first.

'Dance with me?' he said as he swept past the bundled, rounded woman who'd shouted at him earlier. The woman gathered her handbag closer to her chest and, dropping her eyebrows, bristled like a cornered cat. But the man hadn't stopped to await her answer. He spiralled on.

'Dance with me?' he said again. The white-whiskered man crumpled like a paper bag and, head down, began turning one hand over and over again, as though he would find an answer written on his palm.

'Dance with me?' he said a third time, and this time, Kayleigh realised, the request was for her. She felt her blood quicken under her skin and race up into her cheeks. To hide her blush, she stood. If she was going to have to refuse, she would at least do it politely. And there seemed no other choice now but to refuse. She couldn't dance with this man.

He had stopped when she'd risen, thinking perhaps that she would partner him. Kayleigh saw the burgeoning hope on his face: the bend of a smile, the plumping of his cheeks. He gave her a little nod of encouragement. Kayleigh countered it with a shake of her head. And now they were engaged in a routine of their own, a battle of tiny movements. As she shook her head, she watched his eyes dull, like street lights winking out. His hope had been short-lived. The dance fell out of his body: she saw it go. And there was nothing to do then but leave. Kayleigh felt ridiculous, standing opposite this man as though they were preparing for a duel.

She turned to step away. She was thinking, though, of the rent money she needed for next month, and of how she had neglected to save anything much, and of what it would cost to go home to her parents, and of how empty her days would be if she did not return to work. And the thoughts translated into a single unsteady footstep. The dull black of Kayleigh's heel stabbed through the crisp white of the snow, her right foot skidded forward, her left stayed where it was, and as the crunch of her skirt ripping echoed along the platform she was fourteen again, standing on the hockey pitch with a bleeding nose and a swollen eye following a fall which had flicked her skirt up around its own waistband. She rushed to right herself, rocking her feet back together. Her laptop was lying on the snow, but she didn't stoop to lift it straight away. Let it fizzle and blow when the moisture seeped in – she didn't care. Suddenly, she was cold and tired and hungry. The snow looked dirty; the sky angry.

She just wanted to go home.

Pulling her skirt back down over her knees, Kayleigh fought the urge to check how high the rip had gone. She shook her head and ground her teeth together, feeling for the certainty of the grooves. And this time she stepped more slowly, making sure to secure her footing before she transferred her weight. When she was almost at the gates, a shout sounded, but the words were muffled by distance and the wind and Kayleigh was not interested enough to turn and seek them. She hunched her back and continued.

'Excuse me.'

She heard the words the second time, recognised the voice, but she didn't stop. She didn't want to dance.

'Excuse me, Miss. You left your umbrella.'

Kayleigh stopped as the dancing man circled her, his shoes making steady patters on the ground. He stood before her, holding out the umbrella: it shone like a crow's wing in the shifting light.

'Thank you,' she said, taking it from him.

The dancing man smiled, bowed his head, and before Kayleigh

could form another word, turned and strode away. Perhaps he was going to resume his dance. She hoped so. A shadowy sense of responsibility was spreading over her, and she didn't want to see him disheartened. He should dance, if that was what he wanted. They should let him.

Reaching the gate, she turned around to watch, to count his steps again.

She found him standing still on the edge of the platform, his head hung low.

'Wait,' Kayleigh called, the word breaking out without any real warning. It came too loud. The entire stretch of the platform seemed to shudder and shake, like a stage-set in a strong wind. The three remaining passengers lifted their heads to glare at her. It was she who was on display now; she who had to perform. She started walking back in their direction, faster than before.

'I'd like to dance with you,' she said.

They all heard her. She could feel it. They all heard and they all disapproved.

As she drew level with the dancing man, she stopped and smiled up at him. He squinted at her. As she waited for him to respond, she considered the lines that unwound down his face: they deepened into dimples on each cheek. He really was quite beautiful.

'Do you know the dance?' he asked finally.

'I was watching you earlier,' she answered. 'It's *one*, two, three, isn't it?' She acted out the emphasis on the first beat with a curtsey and a nod of her head. 'You can lead. I'll follow.' She held out her arms: one at shoulder height; the other slightly lower, palm open, the way she'd seen it done in the films. The dancing man stepped forward and filled her pose, pulling her closer, and Kayleigh breathed deep. This, she thought, was bravery.

'Okay,' he said. 'Here we go.' He counted quietly into her ear. *One*, two, three. *One*, two, three. And then they took off.

It was easier to follow than she'd imagined. He continued to count and Kayleigh swerved after him, their shoes marking constellations in the snow. Somehow, there was no chance of her slipping now. She was growing in confidence with every step. And as her confidence grew she began to laugh, her head tipping far back to catch the last sprinklings of snow as the dancing man gripped her tight, kept her steady.

'You're doing really well,' he said.

'I know!' Kayleigh called back, breathless with laughter.

The other passengers started shuffling away down the platform towards the gates. They'd given up on the arrival of the train now, though they'd all known long ago it wasn't coming. But Kayleigh didn't see them leave. The platform was spinning into a blur, a hurricane of black and white and iron, punctured only by the flow of her partner's blood-red scarf, and she was laughing like a madwoman, her worries unharnessed as she whirled around and around, the speed of the dance pulling tears from her eyes. Kayleigh was dancing, and it felt just like falling in love.

'Faster,' she cried. 'Let's go faster.' And as they did, she watched the sky revolving above her. The sky, which was brightening now, allowing long strands of sunlight through the gaps in the clouds. The sky she felt she could rise into.

Acknowledgments

'The Glove Maker's Numbers' was shortlisted for the Sunday Times EFG Short Story Award 2015.

'The Dog Track' was broadcast on BBC Radio 4 in 2013 and 2014.

'Salting Home' was Highly Commended in the 2014 Manchester Fiction Prize.

My deepest thanks go to my parents, for their continued and selfless support; to those many, many friends, old and new, who have shown such generous enthusiasm for my writing; to Roshi Fernando, for being a teacher, a reader, and a friend; to Jeremy Osborne, for taking so many chances on young writers, myself included; to those lecturers at Swansea University, particularly Fflur Dafydd and Jon Gower, who have championed my words; to all those involved with the Sunday Times EFG Short Story Award, for making me feel welcome and comfortable when I found myself on a large and frightening stage; and of course to my readers. I hope you all enjoy reading this book as much as I have enjoyed writing it.

ALL THE PLACES WE LIVED

RICHARD OWAIN ROBERTS

WINNER of the
Edge Hill Readers' Choice award

Cosmic Latte

Rachel Trezise

Edgy, finger-on-the-button prose,
Trezise very much speaks for and about
her generation, she is honest, funny,
perceptive and fresh... a first-class writer
The Short Review

PARTHIAN

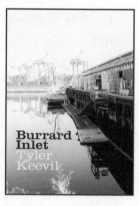

Burrard Inlet
Tyler Keevil

THE MISSING WOMAN
and other stories

Carole Burns

GOLDFISH MEMORY

MONIQUE SCHWITTER

www.parthianbooks.com